JAVA PROTECT

JAVA CUPID SERIES

SOPHIE DAWSON

Java Protect
Java Cupid Series #10

Sophie Dawson

Copyright © 2017
ISBN-13: 978-1-63376-029-5

Dedicated to women who have been victims of spousal abuse. It's my hope that Esme's triumph over her experiences bring understanding of the struggles of women in similar circumstances.

A WORD OF CAUTION

Esme Tobella has been the victim of intense spousal abuse. She suffers from the traumatic memories and scars inflected on her by Hugo Braga, her ex-husband. Hugo's efforts to get Esme back are focused on in the story. Please use caution when reading this novel if you think the topic might distress you.

CHAPTER ONE

Esme Tobella paid close attention to her landlord, Rigs Peris, as he explained how to arm and disarm the security system in her new apartment. She didn't want to set it off at the wrong time and have Rigs and the police storming in, or not have the protection when she needed it. The monitors attached to the wall showing the view of each camera added to her feeling of safety.

"Now, I want you to disarm and arm it so I know you can do it," Rigs said, stepping away from the panel. "I set up your user ID and the password you gave me. That will give you access, not only here, but at the front and rear entrances to the building."

Esme punched in her codes and pressed the buttons. The system clicked and beeped, letting them know it was disarmed. Then, she activated it again.

"Very good." Rigs patted Esme on the shoulder. "Just don't forget the procedure, especially if you come in late at night. I'm not interested in being woken up in the middle of the night, and I know Lori's not. Happened the other night at the jewelry store about 2:30 in the morning. Between me getting there and the police, they were able to apprehend the suspects. Still, Lori wasn't thrilled with my phone going off like a siren, waking her up."

Esme chuckled. "You may want to change that ring tone to something a little less jarring. You don't want your new wife to divorce you because you keep waking her up at night."

"Sometimes she likes to be woken up. Sort of depends on the reason." Rigs grinned.

"I'll bet sirens indicating a security system alarm isn't one of them."

"No, it's not." Rigs grabbed his jacket off a box. "I'll get out of here so you can get settled." He waved a hand at the boxes and bags scattered around the large open space.

"Rigs, I want to thank you again for renting the flat to me. It really helped get me out of a tight spot."

"Hey, Butcher called and said you needed a place to land. I had a place. We SEALS take care of our own. You're his niece. He wanted to help you, so I help you. Besides, if you don't pay your rent I can go beat him up. Fun."

Esme laughed and punched the codes to disarm the system again. Wouldn't do for Rigs to set off his own alarms because she forgot. Not the best way to begin as a renter.

"I'll arm when I leave the building, Esme. I've got some work to do downstairs in my office. If you need help with anything, just call. You can use the intercom if you want."

"Thanks. I'm going to start getting unpacked. Thanks again. Finding a furnished apartment and a job in such a short time... Well, it really helped me out of a tough situation."

"Glad to be of service, Esme." Rigs headed out the door to the staircase, but stuck his head back into the room. "Oh, in a couple of weeks I have a new employee coming. He's still out east. Just getting discharged from the Navy. Wanted to give you a heads-up about a new face going to be around." He closed the door behind him, leaving Esme alone.

She looked around her new home. It was the second story of the Peris Security Systems building. Rigs Peris, former Navy SEAL, had purchased the building, renovating it entirely when he moved his headquarters to Mystery Canyon, Colorado the previous year. He'd combined the two upper story apartments into one living space that spanned the length and width of the building. Rigs lived there until recently, when he'd gotten married.

Now, he and Lori were living in her house until completion of the remodeling being done to the house they purchased.

When Esme had escaped from an abusive relationship and sought safety with her Uncle Butcher in Colorado Springs, she hadn't hoped to find such a secure place to live and a job so quickly. Her uncle had made a few phone calls and suddenly Esme had an interview at Arkansas Valley Hospital. When she'd been offered the job, she accepted, wondering how soon she'd be able to afford an apartment in town so she wouldn't have the hour commute from Colorado Springs to Mystery Canyon.

Uncle Butcher had come through again. He just happened to know someone who might have an apartment to rent. Maybe even be willing to leave some furniture behind. One phone call later and they were heading to Mystery Canyon in Butcher's helicopter. Pretty sweet ride, Esme thought. Rigs had picked them up at the airport and within two hours the lease was signed and they were heading back to the city so she could pack what little she had into her beat up car.

Esme had the weekend to unpack and get settled before she started work in the emergency department at the hospital on Monday. The hospital administrator was delighted to hire her since Esme was a level two trauma nurse. She had far more training and trauma experience than any of the other nurses in the department. He'd warned her that she might be bored with what presented at the ED. Anything above the hospital's certification level was transferred to larger hospitals. Esme didn't care. She just wanted a safe place to live and a job in her field.

Unpacking didn't take long. She didn't have much. Most of her things she'd abandoned in her hurry to leave before Hugo came back. He'd since spent some time in jail for his abuse of her.

Esme went to the grocery store, and when she came back, the building was empty. Rigs left a note on the system panel welcoming her to Mystery Canyon. There was a p.s. that said Lori had told him to say that and he'd forgotten. Didn't want to get in trouble with the wife if she asked.

CHAPTER TWO

Esme Tobella tiptoed down the stairs, skipping the fifth one from the top. It creaked, and she didn't want to let the intruder know she was coming for him. She clutched the banister with one hand and held her baseball bat in the other. It was aluminum and heavy. She wasn't going to risk it breaking when she whomped whoever was moving around on the main floor. She'd been practicing her swings over the past three weeks since she'd moved in. Esme was getting pretty good. At least she thought so. She could swing the thing without grunting now.

She had to skip the thirteenth step down too and nearly lost her balance. It took all she had to keep from falling against the wall or knocking the bat into it. That would blow her cover for sure.

Esme couldn't figure out why somebody would choose

to break into the Peris Security Systems building in the first place. And why they'd do it at this time of the day in the second. 5:43 the time had said on the security monitor showing the hallway downstairs and the man walking along it.

The sight had nearly paralyzed her with fear, but it wasn't Hugo. With that realization, she could breathe again.

Being wrapped in a towel, after her shower, Esme quickly put on a sweatshirt and pants, not bothering to take the time for underwear. She texted Rigs, her landlord and owner of the business, that someone had broken in and not tripped the alarm. He'd get the text, and it would wake him up without waking Lori, his wife. At least she hoped so, on both counts. Flipping the switch to silent, Esme put the phone into her pocket and her feet into slip-on shoes. She hefted the baseball bat and headed out the door.

Now, she stood at the base of the stairs. Her phone vibrated, indicating a text or call. She ignored it. Her heart was pounding in her ears. Sweat was dotting her forehead, and her palms were becoming slick on the handle of the bat. Maybe she should have taken the advice of the salesman and had the thing wrapped with the new sweat-resistant grip tape. She'd liked the red tape. It would have made the bat prettier.

She took a slow deep breath. The man was in the gym

Rigs had set up. He worked out there on a regular basis. That might end when he and Lori moved into their new house. He was setting up a home gym in the bonus room above the garage.

Esme tiptoed across the hall and flattened her back against the wall. She'd seen enough spy movies to know how to sneak up on someone. From her position, when she neared the doorway, Esme could see the man in the mirror covering the wall.

Seems the man was going to try out the equipment before he stole it. He was running the agility ladder that lay on the floor. And he was facing away from her. All she had to do was time it right so he was at the near end when she ran in and smacked him with the bat. That should take him down.

Her phone vibrated again. She ignored it. It would be Rigs telling her he was on his way. Esme hefted the bat to her shoulder and watched as the man sidestepped to the far end of the ladder and began moving the other direction. His back was to her and he was watching his steps. That was good. Especially since there was a mirror on the wall he was facing.

Just as he got to the end, Esme, who'd decided a warrior yell would help by startling him and giving her more confidence and adrenaline strength, burst into the room, swinging the bat as she neared the man.

"What the…"

Mid-swing, her bat stopped its forward progress, caught in a hand attached to an arm corded with muscles. The man must have pivoted as she ran in.

"What do you think you're doing, lady?" The man hollered.

"What do you think you're doing breaking in and stealing Rigs' equipment?" Esme yelled back at him. "Let go of my bat." She jerked to the side, trying to unbalance him. All it did was turn them to the side a little.

"No way. You might try to clobber me again."

"You're right I will." Esme tried to jerk the bat out of his hand. All she got was a strained muscle in the process. "Let go."

The sound of a door slamming shut and running feet had both of them looking toward the door.

"Esme!" Rigs appeared in the doorway. "Stop. It's okay. This is Colt. I told you about him. He's my new employee. I told him he could use the gym. You weren't here when I showed him around the other day."

Esme looked at Colt, then at Rigs, and back at Colt. "Oh. Sorry." She let go of the bat. Colt lifted it high, out of her reach and stepped back out of the ladder.

Rigs came forward and took hold of Esme's shoulders. "Are you all right? You look a bit pale."

She was beginning to tremble. "Adrenaline crash coming."

Colt was at her side in an instant. "Come sit down." He tried to pull her to a weight bench.

"Nope. Gotta walk. Too jittery to sit. Need to let it down slowly. I have work in…" She glanced at the clock on the wall as she began to pace. "Thirty minutes. Twelve-hour shift."

"You sure?" Rigs asked.

"Yep. It's what I do. Pace. Used to it. Happens after working a critical trauma. We all figure out a way to cope." She had her hands on her back, elbows sticking out, as she wove in and out of the equipment. "Some puke. I pace. I used to wear one of those fitness watches until I clocked something like 20K steps in a few hours after a really bad case. Scared me, so I ditched it."

Esme knew she was babbling. That was another way to start coming down from the high. There were other ways too, but those weren't an option. Not after what Hugo had done to her. Maybe never again.

"Here." Rigs held out a bottle of water.

Esme took it, cracked it open, and tipped it up, allowing the cold liquid to slide down her throat. Finally, her thoughts cleared. She focused on Colt. "Look, I'm sorry. I thought you'd broken in. Somehow gotten past the security system."

"No harm done." Colt flexed his left hand, the one that caught the bat. "Just don't attack me again, okay?" He smiled wryly at her.

"Okay." She gave him a sheepish grin. "Maybe, shoot me a text if you plan to come in early to work out. Forewarned is forearmed and all that."

"You seemed forearmed to me." Colt pointed at the bat he'd leaned against the weight bench. "That thing's pretty heavy for you to use."

"I've been practicing swinging it. Building up my strength." She glanced at the clock again. "I gotta go. I need to change and get to work. Good thing the hospital's not far away. I haven't been working there long enough to come in late. Once again, I'm sorry I almost slugged you."

"No harm done."

Esme noted he flexed his hand again.

"YOU SURE THAT HAND'S OKAY?" RIGS ASKED.

"Oh, it'll be sore, for sure, but I don't think anything's broken. Doesn't hurt badly enough." Colt Sawyer grinned. "She didn't swing it as hard as she thought. If she'd have hit my head, sure I would have gone down, but I saw her in the mirror and turned in time. Her rebel yell alerted me, too."

"Glad to hear it." Rigs grinned. "I think we should have made sure Esme knew you and that you might come in early to work out."

"Yeah." Colt chuckled. "Want to work out with me? I haven't finished."

"Sure, it'll be like old times."

They each picked a machine and began working out. "You were the best trainer I had, Rigs. Best man on a team, too. In my opinion, anyway. Jams would disagree, but then he always thought he was the best."

Rigs chuckled. "Yeah, a bit of an egotist, Jams is." They worked out in silence for a while. "Colt, I'm really glad you contacted me when you were getting your discharge. I was thinking about hiring someone. You being a SEAL and one of the men I trained had you at the top of the list as soon as you said you were getting out."

"I really appreciate your support, Rigs. When I was injured, your calls and emails and stuff made me want to fight to recover. You offering me the chance to work with you again, well, it gave me the hope, a reason to keep working to regain my strength."

"Well, we always had a good relationship. I know your skills and work ethic. Makes you attractive as an employee."

"You sure it's not my rugged good looks?" Colt smiled wide, showing his teeth.

"Naw, can't say that it is." They both broke out laughing.

When they completed their workout, Colt flexed his

left hand again. "I think I'll ice this down. Esme might not have done real damage to it, but it is my weaker hand. They tell me it won't ever be as strong as it was; my arm, too."

"Good idea. I need you strong so you can help with the move. The house is nearly ready. Lori wants to move as soon as it is. I've got new gym equipment ordered, and I'll have it in the garage by the time we move." Rigs got bottles of water out of the mini fridge and handed one to Colt. They both slugged the water down.

"Aren't you rad? A gym at home and at the office. Must be nice." Colt threw the empty water bottle at Rigs.

"Just be glad I didn't move this one, or you'd be looking to pay for a gym membership."

"Thanks. It's a great perk. I need to keep up doing the exercises the therapist gave me as well as my regular workouts."

The smile left Rigs' face. "How's the leg doing? Really? Don't give me the bull you tell everyone else."

Colt looked at Rigs in the mirror, then away. "It still pains me some. Maybe always will. Arm and hand do, too." Colt gave a dry laugh. "I can tell when a storm is coming. Low pressure makes me ache."

Rigs laughed. "Me too, and I wasn't ever injured nearly as badly as you."

"Yeah, but you're old." Colt laughed and beat a hasty retreat from the room. "I'm going home to shower and change. Going to get some breakfast, too," he yelled as he went down the hall.

Rigs followed him. "Me too. I left Lori asleep. I'd like to see my bride for a little while this morning before I come back in. Nothing pressing on the schedule. We'll go over more client files when we both get back. How about in an hour?"

"Sounds like a plan."

CHAPTER THREE

Esme walked into the hospital and slid her ID card through the reader two minutes before starting time. She breathed a sigh of relief. She'd made it. Normally, Esme was in the ED by now going over whatever cases were still open with the nurse going off-duty. She hurried down the hall, skipping going to her locker in the women's changing room. She'd stuff her purse and lunch bag under the counter somewhere until break.

The receptionist buzzed her into the department with a "Good morning." Esme just waved her thanks. She swung around the corner heading to the desk and ran smack into a large hard chest.

"Whoa, there, Missy. What's the hurry?" Aaron Trenton, manager of the emergency department and her boss, gripped her by the shoulders, keeping her from falling. He was large, tall, muscular, and black. He was also the sweetest man Esme had ever met.

"I'm sorry. I was almost late, and my adrenaline was still on high. I didn't want to be late. I'm too newly employed. I don't want a late arrival on my time card so soon. How many patients do we have? I need to check with who was on last night? I don't remember? Which rooms are they in? Anything critical?" Esme set her purse and lunch bag on the floor and kicked them into the corner under the desk.

"No patients. Seems it was a quiet night." Aaron studied her. "You all right? You seem a little flustered, or agitated."

Esme rubbed her face. "Had a bit of an incident this morning."

"Not that ex-husband of yours, was it?"

"No, not even close." Esme laughed. "I nearly created work for us."

"What?"

"I saw someone downstairs on the monitor after I showered this morning. I threw on some clothes and took my baseball bat to bean the intruder. It wasn't a break in. It was the new employee of my landlord. He was able to stop me before the bat hit his head." The possible outcome of her swing swamped her. Esme grabbed the rolling chair and sat down heavily. "Cripes, I could have killed him."

Aaron pulled up another chair and sat. He took Esme's hand. "You didn't. Be thankful for that. I do have a question, though. Why did you even go downstairs? You could have called Rigs. That's your landlord, right? Or the police, and stayed upstairs, locked in your apartment. It wasn't up to you to stop the man if he had been a burglar."

"I don't know. I just acted. I didn't think of that. Well, I suppose I did. I texted Rigs before I went downstairs."

Aaron chuckled. "Next time think of it and stay upstairs. Your life and safety aren't worth you trying to be a hero. Let those trained in security deal with those sorts of things. Promise me. I don't want to lose as talented a nurse as you because you did something stupid." Aaron patted her on the cheek.

"I promise."

"Good. Now, even though we don't have any patients, there's work to do. Come on, let's go inventory the crash carts." Aaron stood and turned to head away, but turned back. "So, this new employee. Is he cute? Young?"

"Aaron. I'm not interested."

"Didn't say you were. Well?"

Esme let out a frustrated breath. "Yeah to both. He's cute and looks to be about my age."

"You might want to apologize to him over dinner. Couldn't hurt to make him a friend. You'll probably be seeing him some since he works in the building where you live."

"Aaron," Esme said. "I'm not interested."

"I know, I know. Just saying." He smiled at her and went down the hall to check the crash carts. "Cute scrubs," Aaron called over his shoulder.

Esme glanced down at her owl print scrubs and followed, shaking her head.

Aaron meant well. He'd taken her under his wing when Esme began working at the hospital. He seemed to know that she had a troubled past but never asked. He was quickly becoming a father figure in her life. He was wise and a very good manager of the Emergency Department.

She should probably take his advice and do something for Colt to make up for nearly whomping his head with the bat. She didn't want him up in her apartment though. She didn't know him well enough to be comfortable having him there. Maybe she could bring him a coffee or latte from Java Cupid Coffee Shop. Or a gift card. But she didn't know if he liked coffee. It wouldn't be until later in the week anyway. She was working twelve hour shifts for the next three days. Unless Esme saw him in the early morning as she left for work, she wouldn't see him until her days off.

Colt heard a sound and looked from the computer screen to the door to his office. There was a hand holding a Java Cupid coffee cup. The rest of whoever was holding the cup was hidden behind the wall. Colt grinned. Seems there might be a peace offering coming if the bracelet on the wrist was any indication. That sure wasn't Rigs' hand.

"It's safe. I won't bean you with a bat."

Esme stepped from hiding. One hand was behind her back. "I brought a peace offering. I'm sorry to have nearly killed you with a baseball bat offering. I hope you like Pumpkin Praline Latte."

Colt grimaced. "I'll give it a try." He reached to take the cup from her.

Esme brought her hand from behind her back. It held another cup. "How about black? I figured I'd cover my bases."

"A baseball metaphor, huh? Black's more my style." He took the cup she now held out to him. "You didn't have to bring me a peace offering."

"I wanted to. I'm really sorry for hitting you."

"Forget it. No harm done." He took a sip of the coffee. "Can I give you a little bit of advice? Don't come downstairs if you see someone breaking in. Let the police, Rigs, or me take care of it."

"People keep telling me that." Esme chuckled. "I do like having those monitors on the wall though. Gives me a sense of security."

Colt studied her as she leaned against the wall next to the door sipping her fancy latte. "I'm glad it makes you feel safe." He wondered why she was so insecure. She was living in probably the safest, most secure building in a hundred mile radius.

They continued chatting, getting to know one another a little bit. Rigs had told him she worked in the emergency department at the local hospital as a nurse. "You work, three twelves a week?" he asked.

"Yeah. I take whatever overtime I can, too. That's why it's been so long for me to bring the peace offering. I worked extra days for a woman with sick kids. Not having family or other relationships makes it easy. I can help out others that way. Plus I like the overtime pay."

The back door to the building opened, the sound making Esme jump. Wide-eyed, she looked out into the hall. "Hi, Rigs." The stiffness that he saw wash over her at the sound vanished, her entire body relaxed.

"Hey, guys," Rigs said. "I'm looking for strong backs and weak minds."

"I don't qualify," Esme said, grinning. "I've got a strong mind and weak back. Him, I'm pretty sure you can use…" She pointed at Colt.

"Hey."

"Well, I'm going to draft you both. We're set to move tomorrow." Rigs eyed Esme. "I know you aren't working. You've done your shifts for the week."

"How'd you find that out?"

"I have my ways." Rigs raised and lowered his eyebrows several times. "Actually, I was reviewing video feeds and saw you leaving and coming home each day. One of the perks of owning the security business and the building."

"Maybe I'm working overtime." Esme was grinning so Colt knew she was teasing Rigs.

"You want to stay living in my upstairs?" Rigs smiled back. "You be at my new house at 0730 tomorrow." He pointed at both of them.

"0730? Man, that's early on my day off," Esme complained.

"Tough. Besides, you have four days off coming. Don't complain. I'll supply the coffee."

"I want a Pumpkin Praline Latte."

"Yuck!" Both men said in unison.

CHAPTER FOUR

COLT BOUNDED DOWN THE STAIRS. HE'D JUST SET UP ALL the new equipment in the bonus room above the garage in Rigs' and Lori's new home. He'd been helping with the move all day. Lori's son and daughter and Esme had helped, too. Once all the furniture was in the various rooms, Colt had started bringing the boxes from the garage up to the bonus room and assembling the equipment. If Rigs wanted anything rearranged, Colt would help him. Yeah, they were heavy and awkward to move, but he and Rigs liked a challenge.

Colt wanted to jump down the last few steps but decided not to. He figured his leg could take it but didn't want to push it. He looked at the three bodies sprawled on the floor and Lori and Rigs leaning against each other on the sofa. They were all sweating and looked exhausted.

He stood in the center of the room. "Anything else need to be moved in? I've got all the exercise equipment set up. You've got a killer set of weights there, Rigs. I'm jealous."

Everyone else groaned.

"Sit down, Colt," Rigs said. "You're showing us all up."

"No," said Lori. "Go get us all bottles of water before you sit. I'm too tired to move."

With a huff at their fatigue, Colt jogged into the kitchen. A framed photo and Java Cupid cup caught his attention. They were carefully arranged on a shelf. The photo was of a coral-colored rose at the peak of its bloom. He took the bottles of water from the fridge and went back into the living room.

"Hey, what's with the Java Cupid cup on the shelf? I've always just thrown that sort of thing away," Colt asked as he passed the bottles out.

"That's a very special cup. There's a message on it that helped bring Rigs and me together. It doesn't show unless you have something hot in it. It says, *'Your love is my priority.'*" Lori stretched out on the sofa with her head in Rigs' lap. He began slipping his fingers through her hair.

"Yeah, messages show up on cups every once in a while. They always lead to a couple finding each other and getting their Happily Ever After. No one knows who the Java Cupid is."

"Maybe I should frequent Java Cupid. I could use some of that Happily Ever After," Esme said.

"Me, too," Lori's daughter, Chelsea, said.

Esme's comment made Colt study her while the conversation moved to where the newlyweds were going on their honeymoon. That was the first time she'd ever said anything that hinted at wanting a relationship. Then again, he'd only known her a few days and spoken to her even less. Rigs had told him she'd had a bad marriage and was newly divorced. She'd even taken her maiden name back. That seemed to be a common response of women to really bad marriages.

When Dylan, Lori's son, rolled over onto his stomach, Colt's attention moved back to the conversation. "Speaking of your Bucket List, are you ever going to let us know what and where your tattoo is?"

Rigs smiled wide and replied, "Nope, it's just for me to know those things."

Colt's eyes widened as he looked at his boss's wife. She was close to Rigs' age, which Colt knew was around fifty. Lori was smiling a secretive smile as Rigs pulled her against his side with an arm around her. She certainly didn't look the type to have a tattoo.

A loud rumbling sounded. Everyone looked at Rigs. He placed a hand on his stomach. "Guess it's time to get something to eat." He looked at his watch. "1400 hours.

I'll say it's time. We've been at this since 0730. I'll treat you all to a late lunch at Java Cupid Bar and Grill."

Lori sat up. "Not until I take a shower." She sniffed Rigs. "Not until you do, too."

The rest laughed and agreed. They got up, moaning and groaning, rubbing at stiff muscles.

"I'll go to the office and shower there," Rigs said. "That way you guys." He indicated Lori, Dylan, and Chelsea. "Can shower here. I can ride with Esme."

"Way to invite yourself for a lift, Rigs." Dylan held a fist up for a bump. Rigs laughed and bumped it.

"Is that okay with you, Esme?" he asked.

"Sure, if you don't mind riding in my rattle-trap."

Colt wasn't sure why, but he didn't like the idea of Rigs and Esme alone together in a car. It made no sense. Rigs was newly married, desperately in love with Lori, and old enough to be her father. He watched as his mentor and boss went to the bedroom to gather some clothing to take. Those who would shower here wandered after him.

Colt found himself saying, "I think I'll shower at the office too. When we're all ready, we can all ride to the Cupid together. Help stop global warming by driving fewer vehicles."

"You and Rigs going to shower together to save water, too?" Esme asked with a smirk.

"No, but we're former Navy. We know how to take efficient showers."

Rigs came into the room. "Let's get a move on. My stomach's telling me it's empty." He got their jackets out of the front closet, handing them out.

Colt looked at Esme's car as they left. They'd been so busy he hadn't noticed it before. It was small, old, rusted, and it looked as if the front bumper was held on with baling wire. Rigs stopped his progress around to the passenger side and watched as Esme jerked hard on the door a couple of times before it opened.

"Girl, you need a new car. This thing is definitely a rattle-trap." Rigs shook his head.

Esme just got in and slammed the door... hard. She pushed it open and slammed it again. This time it latched. Colt was walking by the engine as she started the car. Or attempted to. The grinding and a bang made him jump onto the grass. It wasn't as loud, but it sounded like a gunshot.

He leaned down and made eye contact with Rigs, sitting in the passenger seat who nodded. They were of one mind. This car had to go.

"WE'RE TAKING MY CAR," COLT ANNOUNCED WHEN ESME came down the stairs from her apartment. He and Rigs had both showered in the bathroom by the gym and were waiting in Rigs' office. Colt now kept an extra set of clothing in a bag in his car so he didn't need to go to his apartment at the other end of town when he wanted to work out at the office. They'd finished before Esme came down. Colt had short hair and Rigs was bald so neither had to dry theirs like Esme would have.

She was wearing a denim dress that reached to her knees, brown cowboy boots, and an embroidered denim jacket. Her hair caught the bright light from the ceiling fixtures, reflecting it off the shiny black strands.

"But you'll have to come back here to drop me off," Esme said. "I can take my car, even if Rigs doesn't want to ride in it again."

"Not a problem. I can bring you home. It'll give me the opportunity to look over some more files to familiarize myself with them."

All three of them walked down the hall to the back entrance. Rigs held the door open and set the alarm while Colt opened the back door of his SUV for Esme.

"Oh, the girl gets to ride in the back, huh? Sexist much?"

Colt felt his face heat. It hadn't occurred to him to offer her the front seat. So much for him as an equal opportunity man.

"Don't worry. I know Rigs fits up front better."

Thinking fast for a way to make his action look better,

Colt offered, "Maybe I was just trying to protect you. It's safer in the back seat, you know."

Esme looked up at him while she fastened her seat belt. "Uh huh, right." She grinned and pulled the door out of his hand, closing it.

"You really should think about getting a new car. At least new-to-you. That one is definitely a rattle-trap," Colt said as he drove.

"Yeah, Esme. I'll help you find one if you want," Rigs said. "I don't like you going into winter with an unreliable car."

"It's fine, and I have lots of duct tape and baling wire."

"I can't make you do it. You're an adult. You have my phone number. Don't hesitate to call me when your car finally dies." Rigs' voice was flat with certainty.

"I'll give you mine, too," Colt offered. "You can call me if you have car trouble." When no reply came from the back seat, he looked in the rear view mirror. There was a stubborn set to Esme's mouth. She wasn't taking their advice very well. Well, too bad. He would make sure her phone had his number in it before he left her back at her apartment.

Rigs and he exchanged glances. They were experienced with stubbornness. Sometimes you just had to bowl over the attitude to get the job done. There was no way

Colt was going to allow Esme to be vulnerable if he could help it.

He turned into the parking lot and pulled into the space beside Lori's car. She was waiting and gave Rigs a kiss when he helped her from her car. Colt felt a stab of envy as he watched the affection between them. They seemed to have the sort of relationship he wanted with someone. Esme moved through his field of vision, turned, and looked at him. She jerked her head toward the restaurant.

"Come on. I've heard Rigs gets mean if he doesn't get to eat. Is that true? You knew him before." She grinned at him, and looked at the newlyweds.

Colt chuckled and walked beside her. "Yeah. It's a common occurrence with men like us. We get growly when we're hungry." He grinned and grabbed her hand. "Grrrrr. I'm ready for food, especially with someone else buying."

CHAPTER FIVE

"You liking living here in Mystery Canyon?" Colt asked. He and Esme were still at Java Cupid after the others left. Colt had a black coffee sitting in front of him. Esme was sipping her Pumpkin Praline Latte.

"It's better than where I was before," she said. "But that could be more about whom I was with than the place itself." She turned her head away and looked out the window. An aura of despondency settled on her like a cloak.

"I didn't mean to bring up bad memories." He touched her hand that was holding the cup.

She turned back, looking at him. "I know. They were my bad choices." Esme shook her shoulders as if she were shaking something from them. "It's done, and I'm starting over here. To answer your question, I like Mystery

Canyon. It's quaint. Smaller than I'm used to, but that's fine. Plus I'm getting plenty of hours at the hospital. I'm able to pick up some shifts in Pueblo, too."

"You might want to think about cutting back on those with winter coming on. Driving in the dark with that junker you call a car isn't the best of ideas at any time. Driving all the way to Pueblo and back is asking for problems."

The look Esme gave him said she didn't appreciate his advice. "The car gets me where I need to go. It has one big plus. It's paid for. My ex left me with a hefty credit card debt and a low credit score. Every dime I can put to getting that thing paid off is worth it. I'm not sure I could get a loan with the credit rating I have right now. Until that's paid off, I'm going to be working as many hours as I can get."

"I understand. At least let me give you my phone number. That way, if you ever have a problem you can call me."

Esme studied him for a moment. She smiled as she pulled out her phone. "Thank you. It's been a while since anyone wanted to protect me in any way. I appreciate it." Once they exchanged contact information, she said, "Now, you've learned some about me. Your turn. Spill your guts."

"Don't want to. I've had my guts spilled out on the ground before. How about I just tell you about myself?"

Esme laughed. "Okay. Sounds like a good alternative."

"I went through college on a Navy ROTC scholarship. When I graduated, I went straight in the service. Wasn't long before I tried out for the SEALS. That's when I met Rigs. He was a trainer by then. He's a tough guy. Best trainer I had. I was planning on making it to twenty years when an IED put paid to that. I was pretty badly injured." He grinned and held up his left hand. "This arm and hand took quite a bit of reconstruction."

Esme's jaw dropped. "Oh, I'm so sorry. That's the one I hit with the bat. Did I do any damage?" She grabbed his hand and began examining it.

"No, it was sore for a few days, but no real damage done." Esme holding his hand felt good. He didn't pull his away when she stopped studying it.

"Is that when your guts were spilled on the ground?"

"Yeah. Not exactly my guts but close enough." The dark memory made him squeeze her hand. "I was injured badly enough I spent several weeks in the hospital, and more time than I want to remember in rehab." He took a swallow of coffee. "Someone in the unit contacted Rigs. He called or emailed or texted almost every day. It's what kept me going. Kept me out of depression. Or at least not sinking too far down. When I told him my discharge was coming through, he asked if I wanted a job. I grabbed the chance. He's a great guy. Great boss, too. Plus that gym at the office is killer. If you hadn't already been living in the apartment, I'd have taken it too."

She grinned at him. "Sorry."

Colt chuckled. "No, you're not."

"Not really. You're right though, Rigs is a great guy. When Uncle Butcher contacted him, he offered me the apartment for free until I could get a job. The hospital needed an ED nurse. I was hired as soon as I applied and started work right after I moved in. Lori's becoming a good friend, too. We have lunch here every couple of weeks. She's sort of becoming a second mother. Mine's still in Arizona." A shadow of sadness crossed her face.

"Why the sad face?"

"I just miss them, my mom and sisters. It's been nearly two years since I've seen them. The creep, nickname for my ex, wouldn't let me. I can't afford to go, and they can't afford to come here.

"Mom works two jobs. She always has. My sister, Trini, just graduated from college. She got a job as a paralegal and still lives at home. Maria is in college. She wants to be a teacher. She's nearly twenty.

"That's another thing I do. I send my mom money when I can. She deserves to be able to have a new outfit or eat out once in a while. She worked very hard supporting us. I try to pay her back some."

Colt noticed she hadn't mentioned her father. Maybe he wasn't around. Most likely wasn't. "I've got one sister

and one brother. I'm the middle child." He chuckled a
little. "Typical middle child. Not the golden oldest child
or the precious baby. My folks live in Ohio, my brother in
Minnesota, and my sister in Virginia. I don't see them as
often as I'd like. We're too scattered."

They continued to chat about family and experiences
growing up. Colt liked Esme's sense of humor. She was
able to laugh about herself with a dry wit and began
teasing him. He didn't think she noticed that he still held
her hand. He liked holding it. Sort of felt right, their
hands clasped. He thought back to her comment about
wanting a Happily Ever After. He just might be interested
in seeing if he could supply it to her. But then again, if
she knew the full extent of his injuries Esme might not
want him.

Esme kept her hand closed as if she were holding
something. She wanted to keep the feeling of Colt's hand
for as long as she could. She realized what she was doing.
Opening it, she rubbed her palm on the leg of her jeans.

She liked Colt. He was funny and sweet. Turning her
head, she looked out the car window so he couldn't see
her face and cracked a grin. He probably wouldn't like to
be called sweet. Not exactly a SEAL sort of description.

He was handsome too. Wide-shouldered with narrow

hips, Esme knew Colt was very muscular. When she'd nearly beaned him with the bat, the T-shirt he'd had on was tight enough to show muscles on muscles and the ripple of well-defined abs. Short brown hair and unusual silver eyes were framed within an oval face with a strong jaw. Yes, he was good looking. But Esme knew looks could be deceiving. Hugo had been pleasing to look at, but he'd turned out to be a real creep who wanted his own way in everything. She didn't want that again.

Would she like to be in a relationship? It seemed that Colt was willing to explore the possibility. He'd held her hand at the table for a very long time. His grip was strong but not forceful. Not controlling. She'd felt safe. That wasn't something she'd felt in a long time. Maybe never.

Being the oldest, the responsibility for her younger sisters had fallen on Esme's shoulders when she was quite young. Her mother's need to work two jobs kept her away from the house much of the time. There wasn't a time she could remember where she felt safe. That someone would protect her. She had to be the protector for her siblings.

The desire to feel safe was probably what led her to Hugo. She shoved the thought away. No need going there. He was out of her life. Good riddance.

Esme looked at Colt. Even his profile was strong. She felt safe with him. Colt was trained in self-defense. Heck, he was trained in offense. An idea slipped into her mind. Maybe?

"Colt, you know about fighting and such. Would you, um, consider teaching me some self-defense?" She thought fast. There was no way she could pay him. "I'd be willing to fix you a home-cooked meal for each lesson."

Colt glanced at her, before focusing on the road again. "Is there a specific reason you want to learn?"

Esme swallowed. There was and there wasn't. She didn't feel quite safe enough to tell him everything. "It might come in handy someday. There have been a few times in the ED where a patient or family member have become violent. It might be beneficial in those types of situations. Plus it's just a good skill to have as a single woman. Any woman for that matter."

He glanced at her again. "Sure. I'm always up for a good meal. You are a good cook aren't you? I want the food to be equal to the value of my teaching."

"I'm a passable cook. My sisters always ate the meals I fixed without complaint. Of course, if they complained, they would have had to fix food for themselves."

Colt shot her a grin. "I won't ever complain. You just might take a baseball bat to me if I did."

CHAPTER SIX

"You need to put more muscle behind your strike."
Colt stepped back and gave Esme a frustrated look. They
were in the workout room of the Peris Building. Rigs had
set up the gym with a workout area and a sparing space
with a padded floor.

For the past three weeks, they met after Colt's
workday ended on the days Esme had off. He would give
instruction, and they would practice the moves and techniques he thought would work best for her. She wasn't
very big, being small framed and only average height. As
a nurse, she was familiar with the vulnerable areas of a
body. One of his goals was to train Esme's muscle
memory. If she ever needed to use the techniques, she
could do so with little thought.

"But I don't want to hurt you."

Colt laughed. "Not what you wanted the day we met. You were ready and willing to hurt me then."

"That's before I knew you. I thought you were trying to steal something."

"Well, pretend I intend to do you harm. Imagine I want to hurt you. Don't worry about hurting me. I know you're going to take a swing at me so I can duck away. Go with the blow sort of." He made a back and forth sideways motion, showing her what he meant.

Suddenly, he was falling backward, pain shooting through his face, centered on his nose. He could feel blood spurting out. Landing on the floor, he looked up and saw Esme's startled face, her hands covering her mouth.

"Oh, oh. I'm so sorry. Let me get a towel." She ran into the bathroom and was soon back with several face-cloths. "Here, press this to your nose. I'll go get some ice. I'm so sorry."

Colt took the cloths and held them to his nose. Behind the wad of fabric, he grinned. She'd done it. She'd actually hit him hard enough to knock him down. He supposed if he'd really been ready and not trying to convince her to hit him, he wouldn't have ended up on the floor but, still, she'd landed him a good one.

Esme ran back to his side. "I'm so sorry. You said you could duck. You didn't. Let me look at your nose. Is it still bleeding? Do you think it's broken? I'm so sorry."

Colt pressed the fingers of his free hand to her mouth, stopping the flow of words. "It'll be fine. Give me a minute. I don't think it's stopped bleeding yet." He grabbed her hand that was fluttering around touching its fingertips to his cheek, the wad of cloth, his shoulder. "You did good, Esme. You took me off guard and landed a good one. I'm proud of you." He could see tears gathering in her eyes. "Hey, Sweets, don't you cry on me. I'm fine. I may have a couple of black eyes for a few days, but other than that, I'm okay."

Once his nose stopped bleeding, Colt allowed her to examine it. She didn't think it was broken. They'd gone upstairs to her apartment. Now, he was sitting on her sofa, holding the ice pack on his face.

"You know, I can't ever tell my SEAL buddies about getting decked by a skinny girl like you. They'd never let me live it down." Colt grinned at her. Esme was getting bottles of water. When she flopped down beside him, the aroma of stale beer and cigarette smoke wafted around them.

"Sorry about the smell. I got this as part of the divorce settlement. Lucky me." She opened a bottle and handed it to him. "Rigs is going to know. Do you think he'll tell your buddies?"

Colt groaned. "I don't know. Maybe he'll keep my shame to himself."

"I can give you some cover-up makeup to hide any bruises."

He shot her a teasing agonized look. "First, you nearly break my nose, now you want to shame me with wearing makeup? What kind of friend are you, anyway?" He tossed the ice pack onto the coffee table and took a long swig from the water bottle. "You could always kiss it and make it better."

Esme looked at him for a long moment. "Okay, I'll kiss your nose."

When she leaned in to place the kiss, Colt tipped his head up so the kiss landed on his mouth. He wrapped a hand behind her neck to gently hold her to prolong the kiss. Esme jerked away, leaping from the sofa.

Esme jumped from the sofa and stood staring down at Colt. "Why'd you do that? Wrap your hand around my neck." She began pacing. Unconsciously, she wrung her hands around and around.

Colt stood and held his hands out to her. "It's okay. I didn't mean anything by it. I just wanted to kiss you, and my hand went there."

Esme paced some more as her heartbeat slowed back to normal. "I'm sorry. It's not you. It's me."

Colt stepped close and took her hand. "I'm sorry I scared you. You know I didn't mean to, don't you?"

"Yes." Esme looked at their clasped hands. The peaceful, safe feeling she'd had at Java Cupid the day they'd spent so much time talking came to mind. She always felt secure when Colt was around. Even when she was in her apartment and he was downstairs she felt safe. Giving his hand a squeeze, she pulled him back to the sofa. As she sat down, Esme rubbed her free hand down her face.

"Are you okay?" Colt asked as he sat beside her.

"Yeah. The hand on the back of my neck triggered bad stuff from my past." She gave a harsh laugh. "At first, I thought Hugo wrapping his arm around my neck was romantic. His wanting me to feel safe. Instead, it was his need to control me. One of several ways."

Colt kissed the back of Esme's hand. "I want you to always let me know if something I do or say makes you feel uncomfortable. And know one thing: I want you to feel safe with me. I won't ever try to control you or force you to do anything you don't want to do."

"Thank you. I do feel safe with you. Independent but safe. Hugo was always trying to make me do things the way he wanted. If I didn't... Well, let's just say it wasn't pretty. He forced me to do what he wanted one too many times. He left enough evidence I was able to get an Order of Protection. It helped with the divorce. Uncle Butcher helped me get away and find a new place to live."

"Does Hugo know where you are now?" Colt's thumb was slowly stroking the back of Esme's hand.

"I don't think so. I hope not. He said some pretty threatening things the last time I saw him. It was outside the courthouse after the divorce hearing. Unfortunately, no one else heard. After that was when I quit my job and contacted Uncle Butcher. He flew his helicopter to Denver to pick me up. Said I needed to get out of town right now, and he wasn't taking any chances for even one night. He took me back to his place and had some of his friends help get what little I had back to his place. Then, he contacted Rigs. You know the rest."

"Esme, can I put my arm around you? I don't want to make you nervous, but I think you could use a hug. Telling all that has to be difficult." Colt was looking at her with intense compassion.

Smiling weakly, Esme nodded. Her throat was clogged with tears. He was being so very gentle with her. No man in her experience ever had been. Even Uncle Butcher, as much as he'd helped her and loved her, had ordered her around. Sure she needed the help. She had been emotionally drained as well as scared. Still, her uncle had taken over, not really asking if what he'd done was okay with her until it was all over and she was in his house.

Colt wrapped his arms around her and drew her

gently to him. "You let me know if you start feeling nervous or scared."

"I will." Esme didn't feel anything other than safe and cared for. Well, there might be some physical attraction too, but she wasn't ready to acknowledge that. Peace settled around her, and she leaned against his chest. Even when his arms tightened, holding her closer, all it did was increase her sense of security.

They stayed in that position for a long moment. Finally, Colt slipped his fingers under her chin, lifting it so he could see her face. "I'm going to kiss you now, Esme. Fair warning."

"I think I'd like that." Her eyelids drifted down as his mouth closed over hers. Calm and excitement. Peace and desire. The feelings flowed over and around her as they kissed.

When they parted, Colt looked into her eyes. She could see mischief creep in as he smiled at her.

"I won't ever force you to do anything, but I may badger you without mercy about getting a better vehicle."

Esme grabbed a pillow and smacked him with it as she laughed. "Way to spoil a beautiful moment, mister."

"AND THAT'S HOW COLT ENDED UP WITH TWO BLACK eyes."

Lori was laughing as she and Esme were having lunch at Java Cupid a couple of days after she'd smacked Colt's nose with the palm of her hand.

"Oh my. He must have been shocked that you put him on his backside."

"He was. I felt so bad. I offered some cover-up makeup, but he wouldn't take it. I think he considers them some sort of badge of honor."

Lori laughed. "Rigs would be the same. Some kind of 'he-man, look how tough I am statement.'"

"Seems a little backwards. I took him down. Me, a pretty weak little girl."

"Is Esme telling tales on me, Lori?" Colt said as he approached the table where they were sitting. His smile warmed Esme in more ways than one.

"From the look of your face, I'd say what she was telling was the truth." Lori patted his arm.

"What are you doing here, Colt? I thought you guys were on a job," Esme inquired.

Colt swung a chair around and straddled it. "We are. My task, at the moment, is to get food. Rigs' stomach is growling again. Getting take-out. 'Coffee, food, and more coffee,' was the order from the boss."

"You should get him one of those flavored lattes. You could tell him I sent it with all my love." Lori was grinning while she said it.

"I already have two black eyes. I don't want to have

more injuries, thank you anyway."

They all laughed. "You ladies need more coffee? I'll buy. I have the business credit card."

"Caramel Hazelnut Latte," Lori said.

"Pumpkin Praline Latte." Esme grinned at him.

"Yuck." Colt went off to order their drinks with a disgusted look on his face.

"You like him, don't you?" Lori asked.

"Yeah. I do. It scares me some after my experience with Hugo. I'm not going to let that define the rest of my life, though. Colt's so understanding, and I feel, well, safe with him. Like he'd do whatever necessary to keep me safe. I can't really explain it."

"I know what you mean. Rigs makes me feel the same way."

"I'm not going to jump into anything, though. I did with Hugo. I thought he wanted what was best for me. That he'd be there for me. I was wrong, way wrong. All he wanted was someone to control."

Colt returned with two cups. He set them on the table. "Here you go, lovely ladies. My order's ready. Gotta go and feed the hungry growly boss." He turned his focus onto Esme. "Are we on for more self-defense lessons tonight? I could use a home-cooked meal."

"Sure, silly boy. I'm ready to take you down again if you're ready for the fall."

"Ha, you won't catch me off my guard again." With a wave, he went to pick up his order.

Esme picked up her new latte to take a sip.

Lori's eyes got wide. "Look. You got a Cupid cup."

"Huh?" Esme looked down, turning the cup around. Above the sleeve in black ink was writing. *My love will always protect you.* "Did Colt write this?"

"I'll bet if you ask him; he won't know anything about it. That's how it was with Rigs. I got the cup shortly after we met. He had been running and came into Java Cupid. We chatted, and he bought me a Chai Latte. He left, and I noticed the writing. I knew Rigs couldn't have written it. We hardly knew each other.

"The Cupid cups only show up once in a while. The message is written in heat sensitive ink. Once the heat is gone, the words will disappear. You can bring them back up if you put more hot liquid in the cup."

"But who writes it and how do they know who to give it to?" Esme looked at Lori, then back at the words.

"No one knows. Every time they have shown up, the couple gets their Happily Ever After." Lori was grinning at Esme. "Looks like you're in for a great future."

"Lori, that scares me. I don't know if I'm ready for a future with someone. I just got out of a really bad relationship. Colt's a great guy, and I really like him. But I don't know. It just hasn't been long enough."

Lori reached across the table and squeezed Esme's

hand. "No one said you had to settle down and have 2.5 kids right now. Take whatever time you need. Just stay open to the idea that the Java Cupid knows what you need and who can fill it."

"Okay. You're right I don't have to commit to anything or anyone. Besides, he hasn't asked to be more than friends."

"You mean you haven't kissed him?" Lori leaned back in her chair.

Esme felt herself blush. Lori laughed. "I see you have. Well, Colt is a great guy and good looking. Well, he's sort of funny colored right now, all black, blue, green, and yellow around his eyes."

Esme grinned. "Yeah, and now I know how to land him on his rear."

CHAPTER SEVEN

Esme looked at the Java Cupid cup sitting on the nightstand by her bed. She wanted to keep it but didn't want Colt to see it. It gave her hope, but also told her to be careful. She knew what it felt like to feel vulnerable. It was frightening. The cup made her feel vulnerable again. Scared. But it also spoke of something she longed for. The feeling of being protected.

My love will always protect you. She wanted to believe it. To actually have someone who kept her safe. Esme was afraid to believe it. She desperately wanted to believe that the words expressed Colt's feelings.

He was so wonderful. She couldn't believe how he made her feel. He was the first thing she thought of when she woke in the morning and the last before she fell asleep.

Esme knew he wasn't perfect. No one was, but as she thought about the negative traits he had, she realized most of them were petty grievances that her mother called, 'tremendous trifles.'

She wasn't going to tell Colt about the cup. If their relationship became serious, she'd tell him about it. She didn't want their feelings for each other to be influenced by the writing. At least where Colt was concerned.

Her phone beeped. She knew by the ring tone it was Colt texting. She grabbed it, sliding her finger across the screen to activate it.

"Hey, Sweets. Two choices for tonight. Stay in, practice self-defense. Go out for a honkin' big steak. Your choice. I'll pay."

Esme grinned. *"You still have Rigs' credit card, huh? Sure, I don't have any plans."*

"Nope, just my cc. I'll pick you up at 6:30."

Esme sent a thumb's up. Now, she needed to figure out what to wear. Colt had said he wanted a steak. That would mean one of two places in town. Esme went to her closet and looked at her clothes. Man, she needed some new clothes.

Looking at the time on her phone, Esme decided she had time to splurge just a little. There was a resale shop a couple of blocks away. She wouldn't even have to drive. If she could find something new-to-her, it would be great. It would give her a boost of confidence.

How long had it been since she'd purchased something that wasn't an absolute necessity? She couldn't remember. Hugo had kept a tight hold on the money she earned. He'd spent the majority of it. The credit card debt she was responsible for showed he'd spent more.

Forty-five minutes later, Esme was running up the stairs to her apartment. The bag she carried held a new tunic in a dark teal color. She had black leggings, black cowboy boots, and a necklace that would look great with it. Her spirits were high as she unlocked the door.

Her phone cheeped. She pulled it from her pocket, took a look, and nearly dropped it. The number displayed was one she knew well. It was Hugo's. How had he gotten her number? Who had given it to him? Did he know where she was?

Esme set the phone on the table and backed away. There was no way she was going to answer it. The bag with the new tunic sat on the floor by the door. She must have dropped it when she saw who was calling.

With a shaking hand, Esme picked up the bag and took out the tunic. Why did he have to call her now? She'd gone on with her life. She'd met a guy who treated her well.

The thought of Colt stilled the shaking within her. Esme inhaled and held her breath. She let it out slowly. "He's not going to ruin my day. I've got a date with a great guy." Esme continued her monologue as she went in to take a shower. "Colt's even teaching me self-defense. Even if Hugo shows up, I can stop him. Heck, I could even bean him with my baseball bat. I'd love to do that. Well, I guess I couldn't. It's still on top of the lockers in the workout room. Maybe I can get Colt to get it down for me. Or, I'll just climb on a chair to reach it."

THE NEARLY FRANTIC LOOK ON ESME'S FACE WHEN SHE opened the door to her apartment surprised Colt. He stepped in and closed the door. "What's the matter, Sweets?" He wanted to pull her into his arms and hug her to him, but thought it might scare her. Instead, he took her hand, laced their fingers, and brought it to his lips, kissing the back.

"I'm okay. Why do you ask?" Her words were spoken so fast they nearly ran together.

"You look upset. I could tell the moment I saw you. What's happened?" He hadn't noticed it before, but her hand was trembling.

Esme bit her lip. It appeared she was battling about what to tell him, if anything.

"I'm here for you, Sweets. You know that. I can't help you if I don't know what it is."

"Hugo called. I didn't answer. I don't know how he got my new number. I blocked his. He left a voicemail. I haven't listened to it. I'm afraid he'll say he knows where I live and work."

Colt couldn't stop himself. He pulled her against his chest. He held one of her hands and, with his other, began stroking her back. "You're safe. I'm here. He's not going to get to you."

"He might. I don't think the Order of Protection means anything to him. I don't think he cares about it."

"He's not supposed to contact you or come near you, right?"

She nodded.

"So, we can save that voicemail and send it to your attorney. He'll contact the police. They may not arrest him for the call, but they can warn him. It will be recorded that he broke the Order."

"We can?" Esme had snuggled against him and wrapped her arms around him.

"Yes, first thing tomorrow, we'll contact your lawyer."

Esme relaxed against him. Colt released her hand and slipped his under her chin, lifting her head so he could see her face. She was beautiful. Her Hispanic heritage was evident in her features and coloring: tan skin, chocolate eyes, shiny black hair, and thick eyelashes that went on forever. He hated the fear and uncertainty in her expression.

Colt touched his lips to hers. The kiss was gentle, giving. He didn't want it to threaten in any way, even with desire. When she responded, he deepened the kiss. Her arms tightened their hold. His copied.

After several small kisses, they parted, looked at each other, studying each feature. Colt's heart thumped in his chest. He so wanted to say three little words but knew it was too soon. Too soon for her. Not too soon for him.

Colt was in love with her. She was funny, smart, giving, and caring. Her work ethic was strong, as was her personal ethic. She could have filed bankruptcy and gotten out from under the credit card debt. Instead, she was working hard to pay it off. That showed her integrity.

Esme didn't deserve what Hugo had put her through. Colt would do all he could to help her. Keep her safe. He'd protect her to the best of his ability.

Doubt crept in. His abilities were limited by his injuries. He'd never be as able as he had been before. The IED had seen to that. Would Esme want him if she knew the extent of his injuries? Would they make her feel less secure and safe? Would that cause her to turn away from him?

The only way was to reveal all the damage his body had sustained. It was something he couldn't do. Not yet. He couldn't take the chance of her rejecting him because of them. He needed more time to show her that he could do just about anything a man with his skills and training could do. He might not qualify for the Navy anymore, but that didn't mean he was incapable of protecting Esme from any threats.

"Are you all right?" Esme asked, concern filling her eyes. "You looked sad and, I don't know, a bit uncertain there for a moment."

"Yeah, just thinking. I'll talk with Rigs about the call and find out some other things that we might do to help. Is that all right with you?"

"Yes, I just want him out of my life for good."

Colt stepped back, releasing her. "You look beautiful. Let's forget about that call now and go have us a big honkin' steak."

"Sounds good to me." Colt was encouraged when Esme smiled.

CHAPTER EIGHT

Esme pulled out of the parking lot of the hospital in Pueblo. She'd worked third shift in the ED and planned to drive through somewhere and get fast food to eat as she drove back to Mystery Canyon.

As she turned onto the main thoroughfare, something went BANG and her car stopped. In the middle of the intersection. The engine was running, but her car wasn't moving. She shifted to park and back into drive and hit the gas. The engine raced, but the car sat still. She bit back a word she didn't like to think, let alone say.

Someone knocked on the window. "You need some help?"

Esme cranked the window down just a little. "It won't move."

"No, I don't think it will. Looks like your transmission dropped. You're going to need a tow."

Several other men offered to help push the car to the side of the road, out of the way. The man who'd spoken to her before gave her the name of a towing company so she could call.

Esme sat, dejected, along the side of the street. Just what she needed, a repair bill. Looked like the credit card debt was going to take longer to pay off.

She jerked when someone knocked on the window again.

"You called for a tow?" the man asked when she rolled the window down.

"Yes, that was fast. I expected to sit for a lot longer."

"Shop's just a couple of blocks away. Come on. You can ride in the cab. You get in while I load your car. You got someone who can come get you? That thing won't be going anywhere anytime soon."

Esme nodded. She didn't like what she had to do. Both Colt and Rigs had harped on her to get a new car. Maybe hers wouldn't take too much to fix it. She could hope anyway.

"Hi, Colt," Esme said when he answered her call. "Um, could you do me a favor?"

"Sure. If I'm able."

"Would you come pick me up in Pueblo, please? My car just broke down. It's being towed."

"Esme, are you all right? You didn't have an accident, did you?"

"No, I just got off work and was heading home. It stopped in the middle of the intersection."

"I'm on my way."

She could hear Colt telling Rigs what had happened and Rigs yelling that she needed to get a different car.

Esme sat in the waiting room of the auto repair shop. It was dirty and smelled of grease and gas. There were a couple of men with tattoos covering their necks and hands. Esme figured they'd have tattooed sleeves and chests. Seems that one tattoo was never enough.

Esme got a soda from the vending machine and turned to head back to her chair. She nearly dropped the can. Through the window that looked into the repair shop, she could see two of Hugo's biker buddies.

She spun so her back was to the window. What could she do? The shop was in a bad neighborhood. The fence that surrounded the lot went all the way to the street that was a major artery for the city. Cars were going past at about forty-five miles an hour. There was no way she could cross the street or walk along the road to another business.

"Please, please, please, don't let them see me," she muttered as she crossed the room and left the building. She'd wait outside. It had started to drizzle so it wasn't likely they'd leave the warm and dry room and find her.

The roof overhang was minimal and gave little protection from the rain. Esme didn't care. Outside getting damp was preferable to being seen in the waiting room.

It seemed like forever before Colt turned into the parking lot. Esme ran to him when he parked.

"Thank you for coming for me. I don't know what broke. The shop owner just said it was an expensive fix. I told him you would understand whatever was the matter. I haven't got any idea about motors and such."

Colt gave her a quick kiss. "You get in the car. I'll go find out about yours. Why were you standing out in the rain?"

"I'll tell you about it when you come back. It's not good."

Colt peered at her, drawing his eyebrows together and frowning. "Get in. I'll be right back."

Esme watched him enter the building and got into his SUV. Hopefully, Hugo's friends hadn't seen her. What were they doing in Pueblo anyway? They lived in Denver. First, Hugo calls. Now, two of his biker buddies show up a half an hour from where she lived. How many towing companies were in town? Why did she have to call this one? Esme covered her face with her hands. Frustration at the situation and fear warred within her.

The driver door opened causing Esme to jump. Wide-eyed she stared at Colt who climbed in. She breathed a sigh of relief.

Colt started the car and pulled out of the parking lot. "You're not going to like what I did. I'm not going to apologize for it because it was the right thing to do."

Esme looked at him. "What did you do?"

"I sold your car to him for parts."

"WHAT? You sold my car. How could you do that? You don't own it. It's my car. I need it. How am I supposed to get to work? I have a shift here in Pueblo tonight. I'm covering for someone with sick kids." Esme was nearly screeching at him. She trusted him. How could he take control of her life like that?

"I'll bring you over and come get you. I'll take you whenever and wherever you need to go for as long as it takes us to find you a car."

"Why didn't you just get an estimate for the repairs?"

Colt turned into a family style restaurant parking lot. "You haven't had breakfast, have you?"

"No, but take me home. I can't afford to eat out. I have to buy a car. I'll need to go to one of those high interest loan shark type places. I don't think my credit is good enough to get one at a bank."

"I'll pay. Come on."

Esme followed him in. They were seated in a corner booth. Once they ordered, Colt reached across the table and took hold of her hand. "The transmission of your car dropped. The repairs would be several thousand dollars. The car wasn't worth anywhere near that amount. That's why I agreed to the price he was offering. I doubt you'd find a better offer anywhere, and you'd have to pay to have it hauled to wherever that was."

Tears of defeat and frustration clogged Esme's throat. He was right. If it cost even one thousand dollars to fix the car, it was more than its value.

"I understand. It's just… Just been a lousy day."

Colt chuckled. "It's only 8:45. Has it been that bad?"

"Yeah, it has. There was a car accident, a bad one. Multiple severe injuries. One fatality, a four-year-old boy. Well, one so far. There are two people in ICU. Jury is still out on whether they will recover or not.

"I get off work, and my car dies in the middle of the busiest road in town. To top that off, there were two of Hugo's buddies in the work bays of that repair shop. Can you believe it? I don't think they saw me. That's why I was outside. I didn't want them to see me. To top it off, my boyfriend sells my car without even consulting me."

"Ah, Sweets, I'm sorry you are having such a rough day. I wouldn't have sold it if there had been any better choice. But, tell me about these bikers." His tone started sympathetically and shifted to intense concern.

"Hugo's part of this motorcycle club. There are over thirty members. They travel around in a pack. I wasn't around them much. Hugo didn't want any other man around me for fear I might be attracted to one. These two I remember because they have matching tattoos on their necks. I don't know why they would come to Pueblo. They live in Denver."

"I saw those guys. They were loafing against some equipment."

"Did you say my name or give my address out where they could hear?" Panic that Hugo might find her tightened her entire being.

"Um, you want to release my hand before you crush it? That's my weak one." Colt gave her a wry grin.

"I'm sorry. I'm just sort of scared."

"I get that. We went into the office to do the paperwork. Mitch, the owner, closed the door while we made the deal. Unless he says something, I don't think you have to worry about them knowing you were there. When I go to turn over the title tomorrow, I'll be sure to mention you don't want anyone to know whose car it was."

Their food came, and they began eating.

"Esme, would you let me help you buy a car? I can float you the loan at a reasonable rate. Or I'll co-sign for you if that works. My credit is good."

Esme swallowed the lump in her throat, or tried to. "Why would you do that?"

"Well, you said I was your boyfriend. It's just the sort of thing I think a boyfriend should do. It's a way I can help keep you safe. Make sure you are protected. Sort of like a massive self-defense lesson. Make sure you have a decent car so you can make a fast getaway."

Esme laughed. "Sounds like you're planning a heist."

"No, just making sure my girlfriend is safe." He grinned at her. "I like calling you my girlfriend."

"I didn't say I was your girlfriend."

"You said I was your boyfriend, so it's a logical assumption."

Esme couldn't argue with that. She took a sip of her coffee instead.

"So," Colt said. "When are we going car shopping?"

"You seem pretty happy about the prospect."

"I am. I like looking at cars. I'm glad you are getting into a more reliable unit. Are you even a little excited about it?" Colt asked.

"Well, one good thing will come of my buying a new car. You and Rigs will quit harping at me to get one."

"Don't worry. We'll find something else to harp at you about."

"THERE'S MORE TO BUYING A CAR THAN 'OOO, I LIKE THE color' or 'This one's cute,' Esme." Colt made air quotes around her words. They'd been looking for a car for two weeks. Between both their schedules, finding time to shop was a challenge.

Esme had been right about her not being able to get a conventional car loan at a bank. Even with her pay stubs clear back to the time she started working in Mystery Canyon and moonlighting at the Pueblo hospital, and the record of her faithful payments of the credit card debt, each bank had been sorry they couldn't extend her a loan. 'Come back next year when the debt is lower and you have more of a work history in the area.'

Both Colt and Rigs had offered to float Esme the money to purchase a car. Reluctantly, she'd taken them up on the offer. They were going to split the loan in two parts, one for each of them. She'd pay them back on alternating months. Neither man wanted Esme to finance through a used car dealer. They didn't feel it was wise for a beautiful young woman to have to go each month to personally make payments. None of the dealers were in desirable areas of town.

"I don't know anything more about cars than that," Esme said. "I'm relying on you to know whether it's a good car and a good deal or not. You're the man. That's your job." She gave him a cheeky grin.

"So much for women's lib. Come on. Here's one that might work."

Once they'd rejected that car for having high mileage and a high price, Colt said, "Let's get lunch. I'm hungry."

They were in Pueblo, having exhausted the used car lots in Mystery Canyon.

"I like your boss, Aaron. He seems like a good guy," Colt said when they had their food in front of them.

"He is. He's become a good friend. He even invited me to have supper with him and his family. His wife is a great cook. She works at the hospital too, in the kitchen."

"He seems to care about you."

"Aaron cares about all those he works with. He takes an interest in their lives and the challenges of the job. Some people can't take the intense pressure of the Emergency Department. He's real supportive with the stress." Esme took a bite of her sandwich. When she'd swallowed, she said, "He's asked a lot of questions about you. Seems he wanted to be sure you are a quality type of guy. His words."

Colt grinned at her. "What was his conclusion?"

"Once he met you, when you came to pick me up that first day, he said, and I quote, 'He'll do. Keep him.'"

"Well, are you going to take his advice?" Colt stuck a French fry in his mouth.

"At least until I get a new car. He's my loan officer."

He laughed at her comment, and she joined in.

"Seriously, I know I'm frustrating you with my lack of knowledge about cars, but I'm having fun shopping for one with you." She shot him a guilty look. "I may be sabotaging it a little, too. I'm having so much fun with you doing the looking, well, I just don't want it to end. I like you taking me to work, too."

Colt's heart did a flip. Maybe she was more into him than he'd been afraid to hope. He took her hand. "Just because you get a new car doesn't mean we'll stop spending time and having fun together. We are boyfriend and girlfriend after all. There are other things we can do to have fun and be together. We'll just have to find some."

"How about line dancing?"

"What?"

"Line dancing. It's fun and good exercise."

"Um. I don't know. Not really my sort of thing."

Esme stuck out her bottom lip in a fake pout. "Okay for now, but keep it in mind."

Rather than reply, Colt took a bite of his sandwich. He wasn't quite sure he was up for line dancing. An idea struck him. "Hey, after we get you a new car, let's go and see if we can find you a new sofa. Yours stinks of cigarettes and beer."

"I can't afford a new sofa."

"I meant new-to-you. There are several resale furniture stores in Pueblo and Mystery Canyon. We can see if we can find one that doesn't stink. Who knows, maybe they'd even take yours in trade. They could take the smell out and sell it to someone else."

"You know, I'd like to get rid of that thing. It just

reminds me of Hugo every time I sit down and the aroma wafts up."

"Well then, let's plan to start shopping for a new-to-you sofa once we get you that new-to-you car."

Esme grinned at him. "Sounds like a good plan to me."

CHAPTER NINE

"So, do you like your new car?" Aaron asked.

"Yeah, I do. It took a while, but Colt and I finally found one we agreed upon. I thought it was cute, red, the right price, and he thought it was a dependable, cost-effective, good deal for the mileage." Esme deepened her voice when saying the last part.

Aaron chuckled. "Sounds about like the wife and me."

"Well, I'm out of here. I've handed off my patients to Sylvia and made sure all my data is entered into the EMRs. Hey, did I tell you we're going to shop for a new used sofa?"

"No."

"The one I have is from my disaster of a marriage. It

stinks and reminds me of a bad time in my life. Colt and I are going to hit all the used furniture stores."

"Sounds like you're looking forward to it."

"I am. I'll have to take on more shifts both here and in Pueblo to pay for it and my car, but I'll make it work."

Esme changed her work clogs for her cowboy boots, put on her coat, pulled her stocking cap on, grabbed her purse, and headed out the emergency room entrance into the night. Just as she was about to pull her keys out of her pocket, she was grabbed from behind with an arm around her shoulders.

"Come on. We're going for a little ride," A man growled in her ear.

Fear shot through Esme. There had been several women accosted in Mystery Canyon over the past few weeks. He struck in the late evening. Each woman had been assaulted but not killed. Who would have thought the parking lot of the hospital would be the place he found his next victim?

She couldn't think as the man dragged Esme away from her car. She remembered Colt telling her that if she forgot all he had taught her about self-defense, to remember just one word. SING. They'd even watched Miss Congeniality together.

Esme stopped her useless struggling and lifted her arms. It loosened the hold the man had on her shoulders. Bending her elbow, she shifted her hips sideways and brought her arm down hard. Her elbow smashed into his mid-section knocking the air out of his lungs. She lifted her foot and stomped the heel of her cowboy boot onto his instep, scraping it down his leg as it descended.

Those two actions, in such short succession, released Esme from his grasp. She spun around and smashed the palm of her hand upward into his nose. His head went back with a jerk. Blood sprayed, but Esme didn't care. She was used to blood. With the man teetering for balance, her knee came up, blasting him right between the legs.

The man fell to the ground clutching his groin. Esme, furious at what he'd tried to do to her, took a moment to look at him as she caught her breath. She pulled the Kelly locking clamps from the pocket on the leg of her pants and grabbed the man by his septum, squeezing the clamp shut.

"I'm not going for a ride anywhere with you. I'm leading you by the nose to security." She pulled the man behind her to the emergency entrance, him crawling on his knees and screaming as he fought pain in his nose. She hit the buzzer so the receptionist would open the doors.

"Esme? What?" The receptionist could see them on the camera feed.

"Call the police. This man just tried to attack me. Let me in."

The doors opened. Several men, including Aaron

were running toward her. The man she held by the nose was screaming, bleeding, and flailing his arms.

Aaron grabbed Esme, letting the others haul the man inside. "Are you all right? I can't believe you were attacked right in the parking lot."

Esme burrowed into his arms, panting. "I'm okay. I'm okay," she said. Belying her words, she burst into tears.

Aaron helped her into the ED and a treatment room. They could hear the man screaming about abuse. Aaron closed the door. "Let me check you over. Are you sure he didn't hurt you?"

Esme held out her hand. A bruise was forming on the base of her palm. Blood splatters covered it. "I could use an ice pack. I hit him hard."

Aaron went to get one and returned in a couple of minutes. "The police are here. They'll want to talk to you. I've put them off for a little while."

Esme was sitting on an exam bed. She was trembling from shock and adrenaline. Her tears had streaked the blood splatters on her face.

Aaron got a washcloth and gently cleaned her face and hands. "Your coat is going to have to be washed."

"Yeah. I need to walk." Esme jumped off the bed and began pacing the small room. There wasn't much space. When she came to the wall, she smacked it with her palm. "Ouch. That was stupid."

"Give me your phone," Aaron commanded.

"Why?" Esme shot back.

"I'm calling Colt. I don't want you going through this alone, and I can't stay with you; we have an ambulance heading in. Nor do I want you driving home tonight."

Esme grabbed her purse off the bed and dug out her phone. Aaron watched her pace as he found Colt's number and called.

"Hi, Sweets. You off work?"

"Colt, this is Aaron, Esme's boss. She's okay but was attacked in the parking lot."

"What?" Esme could hear the shouted word. Aaron pulled the phone away from his ear.

"She's fine. She fought him off." He chuckled. "Brought him to the ED with a Kelly clamp locked on his nose. She needs you to come get her. I don't want her driving home."

"I'm already in my car. I'll be there in a few minutes."

The call ended, and Aaron put her phone into her purse.

A knock sounded on the door, and Sylvia stuck her head in. "The ambulance is coming in with a possible stoke victim."

Aaron nodded. "You gonna be all right by yourself?"

"Yeah, go on. I'll be fine. And if I know Colt, he'll be here in less than five minutes. Just be sure to have them let him in."

"Will do. I'll stall the cops as long as I can, too."

"Thanks."

With Aaron gone, there was more room to pace. Not much, but she moved every wheeled piece of equipment out of the way and walked in as large a circle as she could. It was hard to believe the last half hour had happened.

A fist hit the door that opened before she could respond. Colt blasted in, and suddenly she was enclosed in his embrace. Her fears rose again and with it tears.

"I was so scared, Colt. I couldn't think. Then, I remembered you telling me to just SING. I did, and it took him down. I clamped him with my Kelly locking clamp on the septum and dragged him to the door."

"All I care about is that you're okay. You are, aren't you? Aaron said you were but…"

"Yeah," she pulled back and held up her hand. "I bruised my hand smashing his nose."

He kissed her palm. "Good girl. You remembered to use your palm instead of your fist. I'm so proud of you."

Esme saw the pride in his eyes. Suddenly, he was kissing her and holding her tightly against him.

"I'm sorry if my squeezing you so hard makes you uncomfortable," he said between kisses. "I just have to know you are safe, and this is the only way I can."

"It's fine. I need to know you're there, too."

When they left the emergency department, Rigs was leaning against the wall with his arms crossed. He straightened and came forward. "Are you okay?" he asked, placing his hands on her shoulders.

"Yeah. Scared, coming down off an adrenaline high, and exhausted, but yeah. What are you doing here?" Esme allowed Rigs to give her a hug.

"Administration called. They wanted the video from the security camera downloaded. The police need it. Besides, Lori would kill me if I didn't make sure you were okay."

"She's mighty fierce." Esme chuckled.

"We're going to get something to eat, Rigs. You want to come with us? The police are done with Esme for now."

"Sure."

Esme left her coat in the car rather than wear it into the restaurant since it was bloodstained. Colt put his arm around her shoulders as they walked into Java Cupid. Soon, they had coffee cups in front of them and were waiting on their food.

"I haven't heard of any Java Cupids in a while. I wonder if the cupid is done sending messages." Rigs lifted his cup and took a sip.

Esme looked at her latte. She hoped she wasn't blushing. No way was she going to say that she had gotten a message from the cupid. Lori knew, but she must not have told Rigs. Esme was glad. As much as she liked Colt, she was gun shy about getting serious. Hugo had been sweet and caring until he got the ring on her finger. She'd take her time with this relationship.

CHAPTER TEN

"We've got an incoming. Female, mid-twenties. Seems she was ironing her blouse while she was wearing it. Not only did she burn her boob, she set the iron down and it burned the bedspread, starting it on fire. Now, she's got smoke inhalation." The dispatcher said.

"Great, another stupid injury." The doctor working the ED in Pueblo rolled his eyes. "I'll be in my office. Buzz me when the ambulance gets here."

Esme was working a day shift in the larger hospital in Pueblo. It was early January, and she was picking up shifts in both hospitals due to sickness of the employees or their children. Being able to work both as a floor nurse and in the ED gave her expanded opportunities for extra shifts. The credit card debt was lowering, and she was able to make regular payments to Colt and Rigs for her car. She and Colt had found her a new sofa. The resale shop owner hadn't wanted her old one so it now had a new home in the dump.

"Here it comes." Eric, the male nurse who was working the shift with her, opened the door to allow the EMTs to wheel the gurney in.

Eric worked with the EMTs to move the girl to the bed. As Eric took vitals and began examining her, Esme entered data from the responders into the computer. The doctor came in, and treatment was started.

When the first rush was over, Esme looked at the woman's face. Her heart skipped a beat. She knew her. It was one of the girlfriends of a biker friend of Hugo's. It was obvious the woman remembered her too. Esme backed up a step.

"Hey, Alicia. I was busy and didn't recognize you until now." Esme didn't know what to do or say.

"Hey, Esme. Long time."

"Yeah. Um, you know I'm not with Hugo anymore, right?"

"Yeah, I heard. He was pretty angry when you left. He ranted for several days. Tore up some stuff at the club. They banned him for a while. He comes back some now."

"Uh, what are you doing in Pueblo?"

"Troy took a job at the water plant here. I'm tending bar. Guess I'm going to miss work tonight, huh?"

"Yeah, I don't think it would be a good idea to be on

your feet all evening. You need to rest and let your lungs heal some. The doctor has released you. Here are your discharge instructions. I'll read them over with you to be sure you understand."

Once Esme was finished with her discharge protocols, she looked at Alicia. She bit her lip. "You know I took an Order of Protection out against Hugo, don't you?"

"Yeah. Jeanine told me how he beat you up the day before you left."

"I don't want Hugo to know where I am. Where I work. Are you going to tell him?"

"No. I won't tell. Not unless Troy asks directly. I don't know why he would though. Why would he ask who my nurse was?"

The tension in Esme diminished. Ever since she'd recognized Alicia, Esme knew her safe haven of Mystery Canyon was in danger. If Alicia wouldn't tell that she'd seen Esme, maybe Hugo wouldn't find out. Her fear wasn't entirely swept away. Only time would do that. There was nothing she could do at the moment. All she could do was trust that Alicia wouldn't tell.

Eric came in. "Some guy named Troy is asking to see you. Shall I send him in?"

Alicia exchanged glances with Esme. "I'll go out. We're done here, right?"

"Ye..yes," Esme said. She knew her voice lacked the

confidence she normally had at work, but there was no way she could speak more strongly.

Alicia, hopped off the bed. "I'll just go meet him out there." She pointed in the general direction of the waiting room. "See you around, Esme."

"Yeah. Glad you weren't hurt any more than you were. Don't try to iron a blouse while you are wearing it again. It's not a good idea."

Alicia chuckled. "Yeah, I learned that."

Eric escorted her out. Esme went to the nurse's station and began finishing the report. Eric came back in and hurried into the exam room Alicia had been in. He came back out with the plastic bag holding her personal items.

When he went out the door into the hallway, Esme looked up, right into the eyes of Alicia's boyfriend, Troy. She turned away and went into the lady's restroom. She was shaking. She was sure Hugo would find out now. There was no way Alicia could keep from telling Troy that Esme was the nurse who treated her.

She'd just have to figure out how to continue. There was the Order of Protection. She hadn't heard from Hugo since she blocked his number. The lawyer had told her that he'd been warned not to try to contact her again.

Esme didn't think Hugo cared about the Order. The only thing he cared about was himself and what he wanted. She didn't think really Hugo wanted her. He just didn't want her to have been the one to leave. If their marriage was going to end, he wanted to be the one to end it. It hurt his pride when she left him. That's all he cared about.

Esme washed her hands and exited the restroom. She still had four hours of her shift to work. She desperately wanted to call Colt. Wanted to hear his voice. Wanted him to come and pick her up. Wanted to get in her car and drive away from Pueblo, Mystery Canyon, and Colorado in general, but she couldn't. She didn't have the money to do that. Plus, she didn't want to leave Colt.

COLT DIDN'T KNOW WHAT HAD HAPPENED, BUT SOMETHING had. Esme was acting strangely. She didn't want to go out. She just wanted to stay in her apartment. She only went out to the store very early in the morning. They spent most evenings when she wasn't working watching TV or movies. She'd even stopped teasing him about going line dancing.

If she thought she was trying to break up with him, it was not working. It wasn't going to work. It didn't seem like she didn't want him around though. When she was leaving work, she always texted him, saying she was coming straight home and did he want to come over. She cooked for him most evenings. Sometimes they'd order pizza. But, when he asked if she wanted to go out to eat, she'd decline, saying she'd rather stay in. It had been going on for several weeks.

Spring was teasing with a warm spell in late February. Colt had thought about getting his motorcycle out. Maybe he could tempt her with a ride. She'd told him once she liked riding. It was one of the only things she had enjoyed doing with Hugo.

Esme wasn't working today. Rigs had left for the day, saying he and Lori were going for a drive through the mountains for the afternoon. Colt stood at the bottom of the stairs debating whether to go home or up the steps. His desire to see Esme made the decision for him.

He knocked on her door.

"Coming."

He heard several locks being disengaged. He drew his eyebrows together. She'd not had that many locks before.

Esme was smiling when she opened the door. "I'm glad you came up. I was hoping you would." She stood on tiptoe and kissed him.

Colt examined the door as he closed it. "Esme, why did you add these two slide bolts onto the door?" He looked at her wanting to see her face as she answered.

"I just thought it might be a good idea. Just more protection in case someone wants to get in." He saw her swallow, as if she was nervous about her answer.

"Who do you think would try to get in?"

"I don't know. Some burglar."

"You live in the most secure building around. It's wired with every kind of security device there is. All the alarms are set to alert Rigs and me if anyone trips them. Who do you think is going to make it this far in?"

"I don't know, but better safe than sorry." Her tone was flippant, but Colt noted some nervousness too. He was about to ask more but the sound of motorcycles coming along the street below, and her reaction, stopped his question.

Esme's eyes went wide. She ran to the window and peeked between the curtains. Until a few weeks ago, they had been open during the day. Colt realized they'd been closed recently. He moved to stand behind her and pulled the curtain aside. There was a stream of motorcycles going by.

Colt glanced at Esme. Her fingers were clenched in the curtains. Her face was pale. He could see her shoulders shaking.

Placing his hands over hers, he enclosed her within his arms. Gently he loosened her grip until the fabric slipped away from her grasp. "Come, sit with me, Esme."

Colt drew her to the sofa and sat down, pulling her onto his lap. He wrapped his arms loosely around her. "Now, tell me what's wrong. Don't give me the 'nothing's wrong, why would you ask that?' I know something's been bothering you for weeks. Is it me? Do you want me to get out of your life?"

"No! No! It's nothing like that." Esme stopped.

She'd realized she had confirmed that something was wrong. Colt waited for her to continue.

"I think Hugo might have found out where I am. I'm scared he has."

"Why do you think he's found you?"

"Alicia, a girlfriend of one of Hugo's biker friends, came into the Pueblo ED. I helped treat her. I asked her not to say anything to Troy. She said she wouldn't, but when she was leaving, I think Troy saw me. If he did, he'd tell Hugo."

"That's why you don't want to go out at all. You're afraid he'll be around and see you."

Esme leaned against him. "Yes. I'm terrified he knows where I live."

"That's why you put more locks on the door and why you ran to the window when you heard the cycles."

"Yes."

"Why didn't you tell me?"

"I didn't want to worry you. There's nothing you can do about it anyway."

"I can hold you when you're scared. I can protect you when you want to go out. I can even take you to and from work if it will make you feel safer. I've done it before. No problem."

Esme just sat on his lap with her head resting on his shoulder.

"Esme, I'll do anything I can to protect you. You're everything to me. There's nothing I won't do to make sure you are safe. If you need me any time, any time at all, just call. I'll be there.

"Don't live your life hidden away because you are scared of Hugo. If he shows up, we can have him arrested. Just because he doesn't care about the Order of Protection, doesn't mean the police don't.

"If he shows up here or at the hospital, we'll have it on video. Peris Security has the contract for both the hospital here and in Pueblo. Do you know how many cameras there are around this place? Rigs tries out every new gadget he gets here in the building. Those cameras don't just show what's going on, they record it all, in high definition, too."

Esme relaxed a little against him. She gave a small giggle. "I've wondered if there were hidden cameras in my bedroom and bathroom. Makes me just a little nervous sometimes thinking about it."

Colt kissed the top of her head. "No cameras in the bedroom or bathroom. None in the apartment at all, so you're safe to wander around all naked if you want."

"Thank you, I think."

"Was that group of bikers part of Hugo's pack?"

"I don't think so. The jackets weren't right. Not the right logo."

"Will you get me a picture of the logo? That way I'll

know what to look for. I'll show Rigs, too." When she started to get up he held her back. "Not yet. It's not important right now. Stay here. I like you on my lap."

They sat quietly for a while. Colt rubbed Esme's back. He wondered if he should tell her of his love for her. He desperately wanted to. His insecurity about his injuries kept him from speaking. Especially now, when she was afraid Hugo might have found her. How could he confess his lack when she was so scared? Until he was sure she wouldn't think less of him as a man, he'd keep his confession of love within himself.

ESME TUCKED HER HEAD UNDER HIS CHIN. SHE FELT SO safe. So protected. Just like the Java Cupid cup had said. *My love will always protect you.* But Colt had never spoken of love. He hadn't mentioned anything about a future with her. And she wanted that future. With him.

Her hand absently stroked the sleeve of his green knit shirt. Esme could feel the strength, the muscles of his arm. She knew how strong he was. She'd watched him work out many times. She'd even tried some of the exercises. Compared to him, she was pretty pathetic.

Colt and Rigs sparred occasionally, wrestling or practicing their martial arts. They knew how to fight. They even knew how to fight dirty. Colt had showed her some moves she could use that weren't considered fair. Esme figured if she needed to use the moves, she wouldn't care if they were 'fair' or not. Especially, if she had to use them against Hugo or one of his buddies.

Esme wanted to say the words. Longed to tell him she loved him. She wouldn't though. Not until he told her of his feelings. She couldn't open herself up for rejection. Didn't think she would survive if he didn't love her back. She'd gone through a lot with Hugo. More than any woman should. But if Colt rejected her love, Esme felt she would simply curl up and die.

CHAPTER ELEVEN

"That's the long and the short of it, Rigs. Esme's terrified to leave her apartment for fear that Hugo will see her and find out where she lives." Colt tossed a couple of photos on the desk. "That's Hugo and the logo of his motorcycle club. I looked them up. They are pretty much petty thieves and thugs. They tend to get into bar fights. Nothing major. Several have gone to jail for burglary and spousal abuse. Seems some of them think women are possessions they can beat up and throw around."

Rigs picked up the photos. "I looked Hugo up when Esme first came to live in the apartment. He's got a record. Nothing major until he beat up Esme. I called a buddy in the Denver PD. He told me there was a juvie record that was sealed when he turned eighteen."

Colt sat down in a chair in front of the desk.

"Has she ever told you how badly she was injured when she finally left him?" Rigs asked.

"No, I don't think I want to know the details. It might make me want to track him down and kill him."

Rigs nodded. He studied the photos some more. He looked at Colt, slouched in the chair. "You told her about…" He waved his hand in the direction of Colt's leg.

"No."

"Why not? If you want her in your life for the long-term, she needs to know."

Colt stood and turned to look out the window. "I know. Rigs, she's scared to death that Hugo will find her. That he'll beat her up again. Esme knows I'll do whatever I can to protect her." He turned and looked at Rigs. "How can I tell her? What if she thinks I can't protect her? That I'm not man enough anymore to be able to."

"You know and I know, you are more capable than most men to protect her. Not only do you have the strength and training, you have the motivation. You're in love with her."

Colt stared at Rigs, silent for a moment. "How'd you know? I haven't told her. Told anyone."

"It's written all over your face every time you look at her. It's evident in the care you take when you walk with her, hold her chair when she sits down. How you hold her hand. Lori has commented on it. She's seen it. She laughs at how you always show up when Esme and she are having lunch together. You always buy them those frou-frou lattes they like so well. Heck, I'm surprised Esme hasn't gotten one of those Java Cupid cups with the message on them."

Colt sat down. "Yeah, I'm in love with her. I want to be with her every minute. Since that's not possible, I want her to be with me every minute we can be together. She's the first thing I think of when I wake up. The last thing when I go to sleep. I dream about her. I'll reach out in the night as if she's lying next to me and I can pull her close."

"Well, why haven't you told her that?"

Colt shot Rigs a frown. "You know why."

"Colt, if that makes her not want you, she's not worthy of you."

"I know."

Colt swung out of his office and into Esme's path as she came in from her shift at the hospital. She was wearing scrubs with butterflies all over them. He wanted to do something other than stay in her apartment again for the evening. He thought he'd come up with a great idea.

"Hey, Sweets."

"Hey. I really need to think of a nickname for you. I don't want you to think I don't care for you."

Colt sauntered up to her side. "Oh, you care for me do you?"

She laughed and pushed him away. "Yeah, like someone cares for a fungus."

"Real sweet, Sweets. I have an idea. There's something I want to try, and I'm wondering if you want to do it with me."

Esme eyed him suspiciously. "What?"

"You've begged me to go line dancing with you. I've decided I'm game. I'll go if you go with me."

"Colt."

"Look, Esme, if Hugo knows where you are, hiding in your apartment isn't the answer. All you are doing is letting him win. Letting him control you like he did when you were married to him. I'm not saying to just throw caution to the wind. But there's no reason for you to stop living and doing the things you want to do."

"I don't know."

"I'll be right by your side the entire time. We'll leave from here and come straight back. I'll make sure the system is armed and working before I go home."

Colt watched the indecision and doubt roll across her face. She looked him up and down.

"You think you're going to wear that to go line dancing in?"

"What's wrong with what I have on?" Colt looked down at his clothes. Navy turtleneck, blue jeans, and military boots.

"Well, here in Colorado, we dance in our cowboy boots, not military boots." Esme spoke in an exaggerated western accent and lifted her hand as if she was tipping a cowboy hat back. "Seems to me, partner, we're gonna have ta make a trip ta the western store an' get y'all rigged out. First on the list is a pair of boots."

Colt stared at her. He swallowed. "Um, Esme, can't I just go in these? How are they any different than cowboy boots?"

"What's wrong? Afraid of changing your shoes?" She grinned at him. Then, her grin faded. "There is something that bothers you. I can tell from your expression. What is it?"

Colt took her hand. "Come in here." He led her into the lounge to the sofa. Once they were sitting, he faced her and held both her hands. "Esme, there's something I need to tell you. I've needed to tell you for a long time, but I've been afraid to. Afraid you'd not want to have me around anymore."

She was studying him, trying to figure out what the problem was. Colt took a deep breath. It was time to get it over with. If she kicked him to the curb he'd go. He might not stay at the curb, but he'd go, at least for a while.

"What is it?"

"When the IED went off, I was injured. You know that. What you don't know is the full extent of my injuries."

"Colt, no matter what they were, it won't matter to me." She squeezed his hands.

"Don't say that until you find out what it was."

"So tell me," Esme said softly.

"When the blast went off, it was on my left. You know about the damage to my hand and arm. What you don't know is that I lost my left foot. I nearly bleed to death before they were able to tourniquet it to stop the bleeding. I'm missing my left leg from about four inches below my knee."

ESME STARED AT COLT. SHE HADN'T HAD A CLUE THAT HE was an amputee. He certainly didn't walk like most of the ones she'd known over the years. His gait was normal. He ran with Rigs several times a week. She'd seen them. He worked out and wrestled with Rigs. There wasn't a time she ever thought his left leg wasn't normal.

He'd been afraid to tell her. Colt thought she wouldn't want him because of his lack of a foot. From the look on his face, he still thought she was going to reject him. Well, she was going to show him that it didn't matter to her. Not one iota.

Esme grabbed his head and brought it to hers. She plastered her mouth against his and held on for dear life. She knew when he got over the shock, because his arms came around her and his mouth began contributing to the kiss.

When they came up for air, Esme punched him in the shoulder.

"Ouch. What was that for?" Colt rubbed his shoulder.

"For thinking something as stupid as a missing foot would turn me against you. How dare you think so little of me. As if I was so shallow. It's insulting." She stuck her nose up and put on a wounded air.

Colt touched her chin, pressing it gently to make it turn so he could see her face. "I'm sorry. I let my fears get hold, and I couldn't seem to fight them off. I've been telling you to get over your fear, and here I am wallowing in mine."

"We're a pair aren't we? I'm scared of my ex, and you're scared I won't accept a one-legged former SEAL. Well, I say we forget them both and get on with our lives."

"Sounds like a good idea to me. There's just one more thing. I've been afraid to tell you this, too."

"What?"

"Esme, I'm in love with you. You don't have to say it back. I understand if…" Her fingers pressed to his lips stopped his words.

"I love you, too. When you never mentioned anything

about the future or how you felt, I was afraid you didn't feel for me like I feel for you. I didn't dare say anything in case it chased you off."

"We've both been letting fear rule our relationship. I say we stop now." Colt stood up and held out a hand to help her. Esme allowed him to pull her to her feet. "I think it's time to go line dancing."

"Nope. It's time to go cowboy boot shopping. I won't be seen dancing with a guy in military boots."

CHAPTER TWELVE

"That is so cool. It's sort of held on by vacuum pressure." Colt sat on Esme's sofa. She was squatting in front of him studying his prosthetic foot. He had pulled up his pant leg and removed his boot. They'd gone to her apartment so she could change out of her work scrubs.

"The sleeve is a special new type that is smooth so it doesn't show through the pant leg. I've got two other feet, too. I don't use them much. One's a sort of springy blade. It's for running and such. You don't use a shoe with it. I'm not much for people seeing that I'm an amputee."

"It's nothing to be ashamed of, Colt. You were injured in a very honorable way."

Colt looked out the window. "I know. I just don't want to be treated differently because I only have one foot. I'm just a regular guy trying to do the best I can at my job. I don't want to be thought of as disabled."

Esme rose and sat beside him. "Well, you sure didn't give me any indication you were missing a foot. I knew the modern prosthetics were much more advanced than previous ones, but I didn't realize just how much. I've seen you run, workout, and wrestle with Rigs. I never had a clue. You two are well matched. I've seen each of you best the other."

Colt leaned back and looked at her. He smiled. "Yeah, it's a real rush to beat Rigs. He was always better than I when he was training me."

Esme's eyes began to twinkle with mischief. "Yeah, well, he is a lot older than you. He's probably getting weaker at his advanced age."

"Hey." Colt tackled her, turning sideways, and knocking her back on the sofa cushions. "I'm pretty good. I win because of my skill." He leaned over her, trapping her between his arms. With an evil grin, he began tickling her. "Right?"

"Stop. Stop. Don't tickle." Esme was laughing and struggling, trying to capture his hands.

"Tell me how great I am. How I'm just as good as Rigs." He was laughing, too.

"You're just as good as Rigs. You're just as good as Rigs."

Colt stopped tickling her. They lay on the sofa

catching their breaths, he looking down at her flushed face. Slowly, he lowered his head and placed his lips on hers. The kiss was long and passionate. She'd been drinking one of her Pumpkin Praline Lattes from Java Cupid. She tasted sweet, spicy, and of coffee.

He lifted away from her. "Yeah, you're pretty good," Esme said. She rolled off the sofa and stood. She took off at a run, heading for the bathroom. "Yeah, you're pretty good— at beating an old guy."

"YOU SAID YOU'D GET COWBOY BOOTS SO WE COULD GO line dancing. This is where they have the best ones at the best price." Esme pulled Colt toward the door to the Western store.

"I still don't understand why I can't wear either my boots or my tennis shoes. What difference does it make what shoes I have on anyway?"

"Quit being a sulky five-year-old. It's all about the atmosphere. If you aren't dressed in the right clothes, you just can't get into the right mode. The proper feel to the music. It makes learning the steps a lot harder."

Colt looked at the wall filled with various styles and colors of cowboy boots. He hadn't realized the variety of leathers the boots could be made of. The range of deco-ration ran from plain to elaborate with all sorts of stitching, colored leather inserts, fringe, and some even had rhinestones.

"I'm not wearing those." He pointed to a pair that were red, white, and blue. The toes were red with white scroll embroidery. White leather covered the arch with rhinestones in blue and red. The shafts were blue with feathers heavily embroidered up the front and back in white thread. White stars graced red leather curving along the top.

Esme grinned. "Are you sure? You were in the military. Those would demonstrate your patriotism."

Colt just looked at her. "No."

"Okay," she laughed. "How about something like this?" The boot she held up was black with parallel stitching across the foot and flame stitching in dark-gray thread up the shaft.

He took the boot and studied it. "Looks okay."

"It's the men's version of my black boots."

"Oh, so you want us to match, huh?"

"Sure, why not? I'd like to show that we're a couple."

"I'll go for the similar boots, but you're not getting me into matching shirts." He began looking among the boxes of boots for the right style and size. "I'll need to try these on. Some won't go on over the fake foot. It doesn't flex quite as well as my real one."

Esme found the right box and Colt sat down to take off his military boots. A salesclerk came over.

"May I help?" she asked, running her eyes over Colt's muscular physique. Esme saw appreciation in the young woman's gaze.

"We're doing fine. He's just going to try these on." Esme's tone was flat.

Colt's attention had been on his task, but her words and the way they were spoken made him glance at her. The pinched appearance of Esme's lips made him look at the salesclerk. She was young, blonde, blue-eyed, and very well endowed. The V-neckline of her blouse revealed more that it covered. Colt slipped his prosthetic into the boot, relieved that it went on easily. Esme handed him the other one, but her eyes didn't meet his. She was focused on the salesclerk hovering near him.

When he had both boots on, Colt stood up. He walked along the aisle away from the salesclerk. He turned around and looked straight at Esme. "How do they look, Sweets? Does my best girl approve?"

Esme's frown turned into a smile. "Yeah, they look good enough to go line dancing in."

"I like that they are a match to yours. It will show everyone we're devoted to each other. I'll change back to my boots. I want to get a couple of Western shirts, too." Colt winked at Esme. To the salesclerk he said, "See, we managed to find the boots I needed. Thanks for wanting to help, but we're able to shop by ourselves."

As they headed to the men's clothing section, Colt

leaned down and whispered in Esme's ear. "You posses-
sive much? I like it."

"You're real athletic. You should do fine. Why are
you so nervous?" Esme tugged on Colt's hand as they
entered the dance studio. It was a Thursday evening in
mid-February. Though they had purchased his boots and
shirts a couple of weeks ago, they hadn't been able to find
the time to take beginning lessons.

They were wearing their matching black boots and
blue jeans. Esme's long-sleeved shirt was a small red and
white plaid with the classic single point yoke and red pearl
snap closures. It wasn't new but still looked sharp and fit
well.

She had teased Colt unmercifully while they looked for
his Western shirt. She'd kept steering him to the retro
versions with lots of floral or flame embroidery, bright
white piping, and curved pocket slits framed in piping with
arrowheads on the ends. He'd nixed that idea, but that
hadn't stopped her having fun pointing each one out to
him. Colt had settled on a blue, grey, and black plaid with
curved yokes and offset points on the pocket flaps. He had
agreed to getting the shirt with its black pearl snaps.

Esme knew how to line dance, but Colt had never

done it. He'd insisted he wanted at least one lesson before he went out in public to attempt it. He didn't want to make a fool of himself.

"I've haven't danced since high school. All that consisted of was holding onto the girl and swaying back and forth. I think I only went to one dance, anyway. It was homecoming my sophomore year. I thought it was boring. I had to dress up in clothes I didn't like and pay for the girl's supper at a restaurant I thought was too expensive. I'd rather have been playing video games in my friend's basement."

Esme laughed. "I'll bet the girl didn't have any better time at the dance than you did. You no doubt had a really bad attitude."

"Yeah, I probably did. She didn't speak to me for two weeks afterwards."

Esme laughed. They were in a large room with six other couples. One couple looked to be in their sixties. The rest were in their late teens to late twenties. "Hey, you suppose we could get Lori and Rigs to line dance? If that couple can do it, they could." She indicated the older couple.

"Lori would, but I think getting Rigs here would be a challenge."

Before Esme could respond, a tall man in a flashy western shirt and snake skin cowboy boots called for attention. There was a woman beside him wearing a dress made of the same fabric as his shirt.

Colt jabbed Esme with his elbow. "See how lame they look," he mumbled out of the side of his mouth. "No way I'm ever going to do that."

"Shush. Listen."

The man introduced himself and his wife as George and Sheri. He went on to explain what line dancing was and giving a little of its history. He called for everyone to line up. When they were positioned as George wanted, he and Sheri demonstrated the steps.

"Your other right, Colt," Esme whispered. Colt had bumped into her going the wrong direction. He switched, making a little growl as he did so.

They were practicing the basic steps which were familiar to Esme. She'd learned to line dance when she was growing up. Colt didn't have a clue. All the different steps and the names got mixed up in his head. Vine. Heel dig. Double heel dig. Shuffle steps. Kick ball turn. Weave. Hitch. Scuffs. Diagonal camel walk. There were more he couldn't remember.

Colt staggered through each type and, just as he started to figure the step out, George would change to a new one.

"Now," George called. "We'll put some together. We'll go slow. Once you have the idea, we'll add the music. You'll find it flows pretty easily then."

"Yeah, right," muttered Colt. He just hoped they weren't going to use all those different steps in one dance.

"I'll guide you." Esme took his hand.

"The first dance we'll do is the Electric Slide. It's one of the most popular and well known line dances," George called. "Five, six, seven, eight. Vine four right. Vine four left. Back four. Step, touch, step, touch, step-quarter turn, brush. Very good. Now we'll do it again, the entire set, two times."

Colt said the steps under his breath along with George as he called them out. He only lost his direction once, stepping forward when he should have gone back.

"Now, we'll add the music."

Colt felt himself break out in a cold sweat.

"Just count," Esme said. "Each step is a beat."

"Count." Colt nodded. He could count. Inspiration struck. In the service, they'd marched to a cadence. He'd find the cadence in the music and use it to help him keep to the beat.

"Five, six, seven, eight. Vine four right. Vine four left. Back four. Step, touch, step, touch, step-quarter-turn, brush."

Colt counted like when he had marched while in the Navy. One, two, three, four. One, two, three, four. It was getting easier. He focused on a spot on the wall in front of him. On the second set, he stumbled on a step behind the other leg. Colt glanced at the others. Everyone, including Esme, had stopped and was staring at him.

"What?"

"You're stomping on every beat," Esme said. "It's like you're marching." Her lips twitched as she fought hard not to smile, or laugh.

"I'm what?"

Esme began to move through the dance steps. Instead of the easy gliding movements of the line dance, she picked up and put down each foot in a forceful motion. She even counted out loud. Rather than the word 'one,' she said, "Hup." Her feet made loud clumping noises with each step. "Hup, two, three, four."

As he watched, Colt recognized his own movements. His lips twitched. It was comical. She was standing ramrod straight. Her arms swung with precision. When she moved one foot behind the other, she tottered slightly, not moving her body from its stiff posture.

When she completed the set, she stopped in front of him. It was obvious she was desperately hoping he wasn't angry. Colt remembered his comment about not wanting to make a fool of himself. Well, it seems he had anyway. But, the entire purpose of them going line dancing was to get her out of her apartment rather than continue to hide there in case Hugo saw her. Since they'd begun planning to go line dancing, through buying the boots and shirts, and tonight's dancing lessons, Esme had been smiling and less tense. For that, he'd take a little humiliation any day.

Colt grabbed her and gave her a hug. "Well, it's a good thing your apartment is large and sparsely furnished. We can practice this in private until I get it right." The smile on her face took away the sting of his embarrassment.

CHAPTER THIRTEEN

COLT AND RIGS WERE RUNNING THE RIVER WALK. THE day was warm so there were many taking advantage of the spring day. They had begun their day early, finishing an installation of a security system. It was mid-afternoon, and they were going to do their workout once they finished their ten miles.

The roar of motorcycles caused Colt to turn and watch their approach. He gritted his teeth as they rolled past. The logo on the leather jackets was the same as in the photos Esme had given him. He took several photos with his phone, making sure he got license plates. He'd run the numbers and see whom they were registered to.

Rigs placed a hand on his shoulder. "We'll keep her safe."

Colt nodded. He had a copy of the Order of Protection. He was going to make sure the police knew of Hugo Braga's connection to the motorcycle gang and that they had been in Mystery Canyon. The police couldn't do anything unless Hugo violated the order. Colt wanted to make sure that if he did, the police knew it and would act accordingly.

"I hate that I'm going to have to tell her. We've been having fun going line dancing. I'm afraid she'll want to go back to hiding in her apartment."

The cycles turned, leaving Colt and Rigs behind. They began jogging again.

"Lori told me about how your dancing has improved over the past weeks. I hear you were pretty awful when you began." Rigs' tone was teasing.

Colt grinned, glancing at his friend and boss. "Yeah, I was. Esme was real patient with me. We practiced a lot in her apartment. I finally relaxed, and it got a lot easier. It was just so different from anything I'd ever done before. Practicing in her apartment helped."

"Yeah, privacy helps," Rigs said.

"You got that right, especially after I made such a fool of myself that first night of lessons."

"I heard." Rigs laughed. "Esme told Lori about it. Maybe the Navy needs to add line dancing to its marching drills."

"Rigs, my embarrassment was worth it. The whole line dancing thing, between the shopping and my first attempt at dancing, brought Esme out of her fear and back into a more normal life. She'd been hiding in her apartment ever since she'd seen that man who she knew from Denver. I had to do something. She's too precious to me to let her succumb to her fear and stop really living."

"I get it. I had to take extreme actions with Lori to make her realize I was committed, and she was the priority in my life."

"What'd you do?" Colt hadn't heard anything about that.

"I broke into her house after she kicked me out. I knew something wasn't right with her reasoning. So, I went back and picked the lock."

Colt chuckled. "That's one way, I suppose. I'll have to remember that if Esme ever tries to lock me out."

"Just be careful. I think she has that baseball bat again. It's not on top of the locker in the workout room anymore."

COLT STARED AT HIS MONITOR. HE'D RUN THE NUMBERS of the license plates on the motorcycles. One had come back as being owned by Hugo Braga. Colt couldn't be sure it was Hugo who had been riding since the man wore a full face helmet. Seems he had some smarts since they weren't required in Colorado.

Now, he had to tell Esme. He didn't want to, but if the man was a danger to her, there was no way Colt wasn't going to let her know. Maybe Hugo wasn't aware Esme lived in Mystery Canyon. Maybe it was just a bunch of guys out for a joy ride on a beautiful spring day. Colt didn't think so. His gut told him differently. There was a reason they'd ridden through town.

Esme would be home from work soon. She was bringing Chinese. Colt rubbed his eyes. He was going to spoil their evening.

Opening his desk drawer, Colt took out a small blue velvet box. He snapped open the lid. Inside was the diamond ring set he'd picked up several days earlier.

It was a solitaire brilliant cut diamond set in a diamond-filled rose gold band. The matching wedding band also had small diamonds all around. He'd been paying on it for several months and finally made the last payment. He thought it ironic that the car payments Esme made to him helped pay for the engagement and wedding rings he was going to give her. He'd been able to loan her the car money, but it had taken his savings, so he'd had to make payments on the rings.

He'd chosen the rose gold for two reasons. First, he thought the pink would look beautiful on her skin. Second, her previous wedding band had been white gold. There was no way he wanted his rings to remind Esme of that disastrous marriage.

Colt stared at the rings, debating whether to ask her to marry him now, with the specter of Hugo looming in the background, or waiting until that situation somehow resolved itself. The last thing he wanted was for her to think he only wanted to marry her because he felt protective of her.

They regularly told each other of their love now. Once that door had opened, there was no way to close it. He knew if they got married she'd be safer since he'd be with her at night. That wasn't the reason he wanted to marry her. Colt didn't want her wondering if he married her simply to protect her. He loved her and wanted that to be one hundred percent the reason they were getting married.

Chuckling to himself, Colt thought of a saying salesmen used. 'Assume the close.' He was assuming she'd say yes when he asked her. Assuming he'd close the deal.

His phone rang. He slid his finger across the screen. "Hello?"

"Colt, it's Aaron Trenton, Esme's boss. You need to get down here. That ex-husband has shown up in the hospital. He's just standing in the hallway staring at the ED doors. Esme's terrified. She's locked herself in the restroom."

As soon as Aaron had identified himself, Colt had bolted out of his chair and headed out. He hollered at Rigs to download the video feeds from the hospital. Smacking the exit bar, Colt hit the back door hard enough for it to bang open. Although he knew Rigs would follow, Colt didn't wait for him. He jumped into his SUV and tore out of the parking lot.

It didn't take him the normal five minutes to get to the hospital. He was just glad there weren't any cops along the way to see him speed by.

Entering through the emergency entrance, Colt saw the man he knew from photos was Hugo Braga. Ignoring him, he ran to the emergency registration desk. He knew the woman working there from when he'd driven Esme to and from work while they were trying to find her a new car. She buzzed him in.

Aaron met him in the hall. Colt glanced at the various trauma rooms. They were all empty. That was good.

"You got here fast. Did you see him?" Aaron asked.

"Yeah, he's leaning against the wall staring at the door. Where's Esme?"

"Still in the restroom. I could unlock it, but I want her to choose to come out. She'd gone to put some papers on the reception desk and saw him. She came back white as a ghost. All she said was, 'Hugo.' I could tell she was terrified. I tried to hold her, to comfort her, but she jerked away and ran into the restroom. She's locked the door. I could hear her crying. That's when I called you."

"Have you called security?" Colt moved to stand near the restroom door.

"He's not done anything to warrant it. He's just standing there. If he stays too long, I can since it's suspicious behavior, but not yet. He could simply be waiting for someone having something done: X-ray, lab tests, that sort of thing."

Colt knocked on the door. He could hear a stifled scream. "Esme, it's Colt. Will you let me in?"

"Is he still out there?"

Colt looked at Aaron. "Yes, Sweets. But he's out in the hall. He can't get in here. Honey, I need to see you. Need to know you're okay. I need to hold you. Please open the door."

The lock snicked. Colt stepped to the side so the door could swing open. It opened just a slit, and Esme peeked out. "See, it's me," he said.

Tears stained her face. Her eyes were swollen and bloodshot from her crying. He could see she was trembling. What had that man done to her? Colt hadn't ever asked for details. He didn't want her to have to go through the agony of relating them.

Esme opened the door and was in his arms. She was trying to burrow into his chest, clinging as if she were drowning. In a way, maybe she was. Drowning in fear and memories.

Colt kissed the top of her head. "I'm here, and I won't let anything happen to you."

The sound of the department doors opening had Esme trying to pull away. He knew she wanted to retreat to the safety behind the locked restroom door. Rigs walked into view.

ESME COULDN'T CONTROL HER TREMBLING. WHEN SHE'D seen Hugo leaning against the corridor wall, staring at the locked door that kept people from wandering into the emergency department, her heart had hit the floor. He'd found her.

She'd known it would happen sometime the day Alicia had shown up in the Pueblo hospital ER. Esme knew the woman's boyfriend had seen her. Alicia might have tried to keep her promise not to tell. Esme knew the methods he might have used to make Alicia confirm it was her. Hugo had used them on her.

She'd dropped the papers on the desk and fled. Aaron had taken one look at her and grabbed her shoulders. "What's wrong?"

"Hugo." It was the only word she could say. Fear and tears clogged her throat. She felt as if she was suffocating.

When Aaron tried to hug her, Esme jerked away. Panic seized her. She ran into the restroom and locked the door. Curling into a ball, she tucked herself under the sink, her head in the corner. She tried to control her breathing, but sobs rose out of her.

What was she going to do? He'd kill her if he ever got near her. He'd told her that several times. Once when they were in the courtroom when she testified at his assault trial. He'd served several months, and she'd been given the Order of Protection. Fat lot of good that was doing.

Aaron called to her, trying to comfort her through the door and urging her to open it. Esme ignored him. The lock was the only thing keeping Hugo from getting to her. Once Aaron quit, Esme just waited in the dark. Despair settled. Hugo was going to get in and finish what he'd started so many months ago. She'd had close to a year away from him. Maybe that's all she deserved. Maybe she should just go out and let Hugo finish what he started.

A knock sounded, making Esme jerk and tremble harder. She pressed her fist to her mouth, stifling the scream that rose.

"Esme, it's Colt. Will you let me in?"

Colt. He was here. He'd promised to protect her. Told her he loved her. He'd demonstrated it in so many ways. He was so gentle with her. Never once, even when they argued, had he made any threatening moves, suggested he would hurt her, or degraded her with words.

"Is he still out there?"

"Yes, Sweets. But he's out in the hall. He can't get in here. Honey, I need to see you. Need to know you're okay. I need to hold you. Please open the door."

Colt was her safe place. Her safe haven. Everything he did showed his care and love.

Esme crawled out from under the sink and stood. She turned the handle and pushed the door open a tiny bit, ready to pull it shut if she saw Hugo.

Colt stood there, concern and love written on his face. "See, it's me."

Esme shoved the door and threw herself against his chest. She wanted to crawl inside him. She'd be safe there. His arms went around her as she sobbed. Lips touched the top of her head.

"I'm here, and I won't let anything happen to you."

Just as she began to relax, she heard the sound of the ED doors opening. Panic set in. Hugo was coming to get her. Esme struggled, trying to get out of Colt's embrace. When Rigs walked into view, she relaxed a little. He was another man who would help protect her. Maybe there was hope.

"I've got the feeds from in here and the hallway down-loading live," Rigs said. "I'm going to call the police and let them know Hugo has violated the Order of Protection. He can be arrested."

"They won't hold him," Esme whispered. "The lawyer said they never do."

"I'll make sure he knows you aren't alone. That we know who and what he's done and that we won't let him hurt you again." Colt's hand rubbed up and down her back.

"You don't understand. If he gets a hold of me, he'll kill me. He nearly did last time." Esme pulled out of his arms. "I'll show you." She went into an exam room and pulled the drape closed when all three men followed. Turning her back, Esme pulled her scrub shirt off. She heard the gasps. Then, she heard two growls. Arms began to come around her from the back.

"Wait." She pulled away and turned.

COLT GROUND HIS TEETH TOGETHER. HE'D LEARNED LONG ago that swearing didn't help. He wanted to spew forth a long string. Instead, he pulled Esme to him and tilted his head so it lay on hers. "Oh, Sweets. I'm so sorry you had to go through all you did."

He'd thought her back was bad. There were cigarette burns, cuts, and what looked like whip marks all over her back. The burns were in the shape of an 'H' as if he were branding her. When she'd turned, the evidence was there that he'd done the same. The scars even disappeared under her bra. On her back and front it was evident they went lower but were covered by her pants.

Aaron picked up her shirt and held it out. Esme pulled from his arms and put her shirt on. Colt drew her back against him when she'd finished. He looked at Rigs. The fierce scowl on the man's face told him that his friend was fighting the same battle he was. Keeping himself from racing into the hall and tearing Hugo Braga apart limb by limb.

"Aaron." Colt recognized the voice as Sylvia's, one of the other nurses. "I came in to cover the rest of Esme's shift. Gretchen called."

Colt felt Esme relax some. "I'll take you home. We'll get your car later." She nodded but didn't step back. He tightened his arms around her.

Sylvia got Esme's coat and purse. After Esme put it on, Sylvia gave her a hug. "I'll cover your next shift too. If you need more time, we can all cover for you. You have enough times for us."

"Thank you," Esme said. She looked at Rigs. "Is he still out there?" He'd gone to look and come back.

"Yes, honey. We'll let him know you aren't alone. That we'll protect you. I've called the police, too. They are sending a couple of squads."

Colt took hold of her shoulders. "I'm going to make

sure he understands what will happen if he comes near you again."

Esme nodded, but it was evident she didn't have much confidence that his words would do any good.

With Esme between him and Rigs, they exited the ED. Colt's arm was around her waist, holding her close. Her hand held on his waist with a death grip. Hugo stood from his slouch against the opposite wall.

"Hey, babe. Long time. You ready to come home now?"

Esme jerked and wrapped her arm more tightly around him.

"She's not ever coming back to you. We saw what you did to her. No man, no worthy man would ever do to a woman what you did to her." Colt's voice was cold and hard.

"You calling me names?"

"Not names," Rigs said. "Description of your character. You don't seem to have much."

"Just stay away from her and no one will get hurt. Or maybe I should clarify so you won't misunderstand simple English. You won't get hurt."

Hugo took up a fighting stance. "You want a piece of me?"

"No," Colt looked him up and down. "I want you in pieces and believe me, I can do it. The law frowns on my doing it though."

"You think you can take me?" Hugo took a step forward, thrusting his chest out. Rigs stepped slightly in front of Esme.

"I don't think it. I know it," Colt said.

"Just know this, Hugo." Rigs' words were ice-cold. "Esme isn't alone and without protection. You come near her or threaten her in any way, there will be pain. Lots of it. Your pain."

"Big words from an old man."

"Take them from a young man, too," Colt said.

"How about we just take this outside and see if you can live up to your big words?" Hugo tried to step closer but Rigs blocked him.

The sliding doors at the end of the hall opened, and two police officers strode in. "Is there a problem, Rigs? We got a call about a disturbance at the hospital?"

"Nothing yet, but it was just about to escalate. This is Esme Tobella. There's an Order of Protection against this man, Hugo Braga. He showed up here with no legitimate reason for being in the hospital. He's been standing here in the hall right outside the ED where she works for…" he glanced at his watch, "well over an hour. Seems a bit suspicious to me."

The policemen looked at Hugo. "An Order of Protection, huh?"

"Yes, I took it to the station myself, so it would be on record," Rigs said.

"And you are?" The police officer looked at Colt.

"Colt Sawyer. I'm Esme's boyfriend."

"Is that true?" The officer looked at Esme.

"Yes." The word was softly spoken.

The officer focused on Hugo. "Let me see your identification, please." Hugo pulled out his wallet and handed over his driver's license. "I see you're from Denver. So, what are you doing here? You needing medical treatment? Picking someone up?"

Colt could tell Hugo was just about to lie. "Whatever excuse you come up with is easily verifiable."

Hugo shot him a hate-filled look. "I wanted to see Esme. We were married, and I'm wanting to get back together."

Esme pressed herself against Colt. He tucked her closer under his arm.

"You're in violation of the Order, Mr. Braga." The officer said. "Doesn't matter what you want. You've been ordered by the court to stay away. Now, I can arrest you for that violation, or you can go back to Denver and stay away from Mystery Canyon and your ex-wife."

Hugo studied the officers, then scanned Rigs and Colt. Shifting his focus to Esme, he said, "Until later, babe." He turned and walked to the exit followed by one of the officers.

The officer held a business card out toward Esme. She made no move to take it. He handed it to Rigs. "Give this to Ms. Tobella. I'll be sure to link the O of P to my report. I'm sorry you had to go through this, Ms. Tobella. Contact me if there's anything I can do for you."

"I will." Esme whispered.

The other officer came back in. "Chet and Mike are following him out of town. Hopefully, he won't come back."

"Thanks, guys," Rigs said.

"Anytime, Rigs."

CHAPTER FOURTEEN

"You go shower and get into some comfy clothes. I'll scramble some eggs. You have bacon?" Colt helped Esme remove her coat. They were in her apartment. Rigs was downstairs. He'd said he was going to review the video of the hallway.

Esme nodded and went to her bedroom. Colt watched as she gathered some sleep pants, a loose T-shirt, and underwear. Once she'd closed herself in the bathroom, he sank down on the sofa. He ran his hands through his hair.

The extent of her scarring had astounded him. They made him a bit nauseous. He knew she was scared of Hugo, but now he understood just how terrified she must be. How was he going to keep her safe? He knew Hugo wasn't going to stop coming after her. That letter he'd burned into Esme's skin said he thought he owned her.

Colt wanted to wrap her in bubble wrap and hide her away. He thought of them just picking up and moving to another state. That would just mean Hugo won. That he still controlled Esme. That's what abuse actually was—power and control over someone else.

They both had good jobs. They were making some new friends. Going to the church Rigs and Lori went to helped them in becoming part of the community. He didn't want to leave Mystery Canyon. It was a good town, a welcoming place with good people.

Colt heard the shower stop running and got up. He needed to get to fixing the food. He put bacon on a rack and set it to cooking in the microwave. There was bread he could toast. Eggs, cheese, and butter turned into omelets as Esme came out of the bathroom. He wanted to laugh at what she wore but the sadness, doubt, and uncertainty kept him from it.

"That smells good." Esme came over and began to make coffee.

They got the meal onto the table and sat down. Colt took a bite and looked at Esme. She was just sitting, staring at her plate. He reached across and took hold of her hand. "I know you're scared and upset, but you need to eat. After that, I want you to take a nap. All the emotions of the day must have exhausted you."

Terrified eyes shot to his. "I don't want to be alone."

"I'll stay right here for as long as you want. Rigs is

downstairs. The security system is armed. The police escorted Hugo out of town."

"He'll come back."

"Maybe, but not today. The police will be watching for him, and he'll know it. Now eat."

She cracked a weak grin at him. "Is that an order?"

"Yes." He took another bite of his eggs and smiled when she picked up her fork and began eating.

"DON'T LEAVE ME." ESME GRABBED COLT'S HAND. HE was standing beside her bed where he'd just tucked her in.

"I'm not, Sweets. I'm just going to do the dishes, and I'll watch some TV or something. Maybe I'll have Rigs bring up my laptop. I could get some work done."

"No, don't leave me alone in here. I can't..." She didn't know what she couldn't do, but panic was beginning to rise, gripping her chest and threatening to close her throat. "Please, I need you to hold me."

Colt looked down at her. Indecision was evident in his expression. "You sure?"

"Just hold me Colt. Nothing more. I just can't be alone right now. I wouldn't be able to close my eyes."

"Okay." He went around the bed and sat down, taking off his boots.

When he slipped under the blankets, the panic began

to recede. As he snuggled against her back and wrapped an arm around her, Esme began to relax. Within moments, exhaustion hit. "I think I can sleep now."

"You go right ahead. I'm here, I love you, and will always protect you."

"Just like on the Java Cupid cup." Esme didn't realize she'd vocalized her thought as she fell asleep.

COLT LAY HOLDING ESME WHILE SHE SLEPT. HE THOUGHT about her words. "Just like on the Java Cupid cup." Had she gotten one of the cups with a message? He looked over her head and saw one sitting on the nightstand. Curiosity got the better of him.

Knowing she'd sleep for quite a while, Colt got out of bed and picked up the cup. Going to the kitchen, he filled the cup with hot coffee. Soon, letters appeared as the heat activated the ink. *'My love will always protect you.'*

When had she gotten it? Why hadn't she told him about it? Okay, he understood. It wasn't something you brought up in normal conversation. 'Hey, guess what. I got a message from the Java Cupid.' Still, they were very close. They'd confessed their love for each other. Colt had engagement and wedding rings in his desk downstairs. Esme didn't know that, but still.

Absentmindedly, he took a sip. Colt grimaced and

looked at the liquid. It was some flavored coffee. He walked to the sink and poured it down the drain. Rinsing the cup with cold water, he saw the letters fade away.

The writing may have disappeared but the message hadn't. He was in love with Esme, and he'd do everything he could to protect her. There was something he could do that would help with that. Help her by being near her most of the time.

Colt went back into the bedroom and set the Java Cupid cup on the nightstand. He stood next to the bed and watched her for a long moment. She slept peacefully. He'd take a moment and run downstairs to get a few things. He didn't want to be gone long enough for her to wake up with him not there.

It didn't take him long to get the items he wanted to take upstairs. Colt stopped in Rigs' office before going back up to her apartment.

"Hey, how's she doing?" his boss asked.

"She's asleep. I'm taking my laptop and going back up. I don't want her to wake up alone. I'll get some work done in the meantime."

"Not a problem. I didn't figure you'd get much accomplished today."

Colt chuckled. "I'd go stir-crazy just sitting there. I don't have a clue as to how long she'll sleep. That whole thing was extremely stressful." He glanced out the office door eyeing the base of the staircase. "Rigs, did you know she got a message from the Java Cupid?"

"No." Rigs shook his head.

"*'My love will always protect you.'* That's what it said. Just like Lori, she kept the cup."

"How'd you find out?" Rigs leaned back in his chair.

"Esme murmured about it as she drifted off to sleep. The cup was on her nightstand. I filled it with coffee, some awful flavored stuff, and the message appeared."

Rigs grinned at his commentary about the coffee. "You're more than capable of protecting her, and you have me as back-up. She's like a daughter to me."

"I know and thanks. I'll do whatever I can to not only make sure she's safe and protected physically, but her emotions and mental state, too."

Rigs nodded. "Get out of here and back upstairs to her. I'll text you when I'm heading out. Oh, I think Lori's planning on bringing supper over, so plan for company later."

"Okay, thanks." Colt left the office. A moment later he poked his head back in. "Oh, just to let you know, she has that baseball bat with her again. She must have gotten it down herself. I plan to ask her about it." He grinned.

The sound of Rigs laughing followed Colt up the stairs.

Tapping sounds filtered in as Esme came awake. They quit as she rolled onto her back and opened her eyes. Colt was sitting next to her on the bed with his laptop on his lap. He closed the lid and tossed it to the end of the bed. He slid down so he was lying next to her and drew her near with an arm around her.

"Hey, did you sleep well?"

"Yeah, I think so." Esme stretched. "Thanks for staying."

"Sweets, I wasn't going to leave you. Sure, I ran downstairs and got my laptop, but that's as far as I went.

"Rigs said Lori is bringing supper for you, or rather us. They'll probably eat here too. No, don't get up." Colt pressed her down when she began to get out of bed. "I picked up. I did the dishes and straightened everything. You should be proud of me. I even set the table."

Esme relaxed. "Lori and Rigs wouldn't care anyway, would they?"

"No, they wouldn't. I knew you would, so I did what I could. You'll probably find something I missed, but don't worry about it now. Just relax. Besides, I like lying here with you. I'd like to do it more often."

Esme didn't say anything. He was alluding to something, but she didn't want to hope. Colt pulled on her so she turned on her side to face him. He was lying on top of the covers.

"Esme, you know I love you. I want to be there for

you all the time. Not simply to protect you, but for everything. For all the fun and laughter. For the boring everyday stuff. For all the challenges and tough times. I just want to be with you."

Esme took in his intense, serious expression. Was he leading up to something? She certainly hoped so.

"I wanted this to be a really romantic setting. To have the only thing involved be our love for each other. I could wait and try to set that up, but…" He paused. "Esme, I love you so much. Will you marry me?"

Her throat was clogged. No sound was going to make it past the tears. She nodded. Colt must have known she was overcome with her feelings. He smiled and brought his lips to hers.

"Thank you," he murmured against her mouth.

Finally, Esme's throat cleared enough for her to whisper; their lips still pressed together. "I love you."

"I love you, too," Colt replied. He stopped further conversation as he deepened the kiss, much to Esme's delight.

She was disappointed when he finally pulled back. Colt studied her face before he rolled away.

"Stay right there. We aren't done yet." He rolled back and held a small navy velvet box in his hand. "I put this on layaway a while back. I just got it out of hawk. Like I said, I wanted to ask and give this to you in some romantic way."

Esme pressed shaking fingers to his lips. "This is perfect."

Colt handed the box to her. "I hope you like it."

Esme could barely hold onto the small box, her hands were trembling so. When she finally succeeded in opening it, the tears that had threatened rolled down her cheeks. "Oh, it's beautiful." She touched the diamond ring then the wedding band.

"Not as beautiful as you are."

Esme touched his cheek with her fingertips, and carefully took the engagement ring out of the slot. "Will you put it on my finger?"

Colt took the ring, leaned close, and kissed her long and slow. "Give me your left hand, please."

When she did, Colt brought it to his lips, kissed each finger He slipped the ring on the fourth one. "There, we are officially engaged." Their mouths met, yet again. When they parted, Colt's eyes began to twinkle. "I never thought I'd propose to someone wearing an Elmo T-shirt and Tweety Bird pants."

CHAPTER FIFTEEN

"It's beautiful, Esme," Lori said as she examined the ring. "So, have you talked about a date for the wedding?" They were sitting on the sofa in Esme's apartment. After Lori and Rigs arrived with lasagna, the men left to check on a signal from one of their installed systems.

"Colt doesn't want to wait very long." She grinned. "He has two reasons. I'm sure you can guess what one is."

Lori chuckled. "Of course I can. He's a man isn't he?"

"Yeah." Esme laughed, too. Her smile faded and she sobered. "The other reason is because of Hugo. Colt knows I'm scared to stay here alone. We want to start off right in our marriage and don't want to live together before. It's a mistake I made last time. It might not have changed anything, but if I'd waited and gotten to know

Hugo better, how he was, maybe I would have ditched him a lot earlier. He would probably have shown what a jerk he was. It's much more difficult to get out when you're living with someone."

Lori nodded. "I understand his concern and yours, too. I have an idea. How about you come and stay with us until you two get married? We have room."

"I appreciate the offer, but I don't want to impose." Esme got up and went to look at the monitors showing the video from the security cameras around the Peris building. "I don't know how long it will be before the wedding."

"Not a problem. But, if you guys don't want a fancy wedding, you could always go to the courthouse."

"Here come Colt and Rigs. Let's get the food out."

The men came in, and each woman received a kiss. Soon, they were seated and dishing up Lori's lasagna. Esme had made a salad and garlic bread.

"Rigs," Lori said. "I invited Esme to stay with us until she and Colt get married."

"Fine with me. We have room." He looked at Esme. "I'd feel better with you at the house rather than here alone."

"Colt," Esme said. "What kind of wedding do you want? I don't care. I've done the white wedding thing."

"I don't care either. I just don't want it to take long. The sooner the better for me."

Lori and Esme started laughing.

"What?" Colt looked confused.

"Never mind." Lori patted his arm. "I suggested you could just go to the courthouse."

"No." Rigs said. Everyone looked at him. "It would show up in the newspaper under the legals. That would tip Hugo off."

"We don't want to do that," Esme said.

"I suggest going to Vegas." Rigs grinned. "We could fly there and have a couple days to celebrate. You're all legally wed, and it's not posted anywhere Hugo might see."

"That's a great idea," Colt said at the same time Esme asked, "We?"

Rigs smiled a wide smile at her. "You gotta have someone give you away. That's me. I'm the best man, too. You need a wedding planner and a matron of honor. That's Lori."

"Great idea," Lori said, excitement evident in her expression and voice. "Esme, you and I will look for a dress for you tomorrow. Rigs and Colt can make the arrangements."

"But…" Esme started.

"I think it's a great idea, too." Colt touched Esme's cheek. "I can't wait to have you as my wife. I love you."

"I love you, too. It's just happening so fast. This morning Hugo shows up. This afternoon, you propose.

Tomorrow, I'm supposed to look for a dress to get married in. In a couple of days, we fly to Vegas and get married." Esme gaped at Colt, her eyes wide as doubts assailed her.

Colt stood and pulled her from her chair into his arms. "If it's too sudden, we'll wait. I get that it seems bizarre. A lot has happened today. I don't want you to be pressured into doing something you're uncomfortable with. I love you too much to try to convince you. When you're ready, we'll get married." He kissed her forehead. "I would like you to stay with Rigs and Lori until we get married though. I can't protect you if I'm across town."

Esme relaxed against him. The sudden fear that she was being forced into a quickie wedding faded with his words. She tipped her head back so she could see his face. The love and concern for her was evident. "I will, but it won't be long. You just showed how much you value me by not insisting we get married right now. It's not something I'm used to. Being listened to and considered." Esme stood on tiptoe and kissed him. "Sylvia is covering my next couple of shifts. They're my last for four days. I say we take those days and get married." She looked at Rigs and Lori. "Well, seems we all have lots to do tomorrow if we are flying to Vegas ASAP. I say we finish eating, and you guys," she pointed to Rigs and Colt, "do the dishes while Lori and I pack what I'll need not only for tonight but for our trip."

COLT'S HEART WAS RACING. IN A FEW MOMENTS, ESME would enter the wedding chapel. Two days ago, while she and Lori went dress shopping, he and Rigs booked the flights, a hotel, and rented a car. A search for a wedding chapel was also done. There would be no cheesy Elvis officiating their ceremony.

They'd flown to Vegas early the following morning. Lori had appointments for herself and Esme at a spa where they would get the full treatment of massages, facials, hair, nails, and makeup. Esme had protested that she couldn't afford it, but Lori insisted it was her wedding gift to the bride. Well, the groom too, since he'd benefit from the treatments Esme enjoyed.

It was sad that neither of their families were able to come to the wedding on such short notice. They'd called Esme's mother and his parents after she had packed to spend the night with Rigs and Lori. When time permitted, they would drive to Arizona to see Esme's family. They planned to visit his sometime during the holiday season.

Rigs had suggested he and Colt wear their Navy uniforms. Colt grabbed the idea since he didn't own a suit and wasn't looking forward to renting a tuxedo.

The canned music in the chapel changed to some classical piece— he hadn't a clue what it was called. Colt didn't care. All he wanted was for the doors to open and see Esme walking toward him.

Lori came through first. Rigs had told him his wife would be wearing the dress she wore for their wedding. Colt kept his eyes trained on the door as Lori walked up the aisle. The doors closed again. Colt wanted to tap his foot in frustration but was able to restrain his impatience. Finally, the doors opened, and his bride stood there. Her beauty stole his breath.

Esme's midnight black hair fell in great waves across her shoulders. The dress was a deep ruby red, with a square neck, and short sleeves. It hugged her torso before flaring into a wide skirt to her knees. He didn't know much about women's clothing. All he knew was that she was walking toward him with a beautiful smile on her face.

Colt stepped forward, meeting her as she approached. "You look lovely." His compliment caused color to bloom on her cheeks.

"Thank you. You clean up pretty well yourself."

"Come." He turned, offering her his arm. "Let's get married."

Colt wasn't sure what he said in his vows. He must have responded at the proper times with the right words. He did remember when the minister said, "I now pronounce you husband and wife. You may kiss your bride."

He did, enthusiastically.

THEY SPENT THE NEXT THREE DAYS ENJOYING LAS VEGAS. Esme and Colt spent most of the first day in their hotel room. Rigs teased them unmercifully when they met for supper, until Lori made him stop.

Esme didn't care. She was happy. Colt was a wonderful, giving lover. He gave her something Hugo never had: value. It wasn't all about him. Colt's attitude toward her made Esme want to show her love to him.

Esme wasn't interested in the casinos. She didn't have money to throw away in a machine or at a table. Since they'd rented a car, the four of them headed out of town and toured the Hoover Dam. They checked out Fremont Street. Rigs and Colt rode race cars while the ladies watched. Esme and Lori made the men take them shopping. It was window shopping, but neither one cared. They ate too much, sunbathed beside the hotel pool, and laughed.

To Esme, it was a wonderful honeymoon, even if it only lasted three days.

"PAYBACKS, RIGS, PAYBACKS." COLT WAS ON THE LOWER

end of the mattress he and Rigs were maneuvering up the staircase. They'd already carried the boxsprings and frame into the apartment. Colt had purchased the King-size bed when he moved to Mystery Canyon. Esme's bed was small, second-hand, and sagged. The decision to get rid of it was an easy one.

"Yeah, but when you helped Lori and me move, we didn't have to haul stuff down and to the dump."

"Hey, I carried all that workout equipment up to the bonus room. That included a full set of weights."

"Quit your bickering, guys." Lori said from the top of the stairs. "It's not like you're moving an entire house. It's only a few pieces of furniture." Most of what Colt had came with the apartment so were left behind.

They'd come home from Las Vegas on a morning flight and decided to move Colt into Esme's apartment that day. Or at least the bed and few other pieces he had. Esme and Lori packed his clothing. They didn't need to get everything moved that day as Colt had possession of the place until the first of the month. The plan was to move the necessities today. The newlyweds would move the rest over the next couple of weeks as their schedules allowed.

Esme and Lori made the bed once it was set up.

"We need a new dresser," Colt said. "There's not enough room in this one for my clothes."

"You're going to need a nightstand. There's only one.

It's pretty pathetic, too." Rigs nudged the plastic three-drawer storage unit with the small desk lamp and digital clock sitting on it.

"Hugo got the bedroom set. I sure didn't want it," Esme said.

Colt came over and hugged her. "I'm glad. We can get the furniture we need as we want. It's worked for you so far. A while longer won't matter." He kissed her.

Esme smiled. "Yeah, I like shopping with you. You've helped me buy a new sofa and car, after you sold my old one," she teased.

"Something that desperately needed to be done," Rigs mumbled.

"Okay, mister. Let's get out of here and leave the newlyweds alone. They haven't had any time to themselves since they got married." Lori grabbed Rigs' hand, pulling him to the door.

"They were alone part of the time. I sure wasn't in the hotel room with them."

"Say goodbye, Rigs," Lori deadpanned.

"Goodbye, Rigs," he said.

Colt kept his arm around Esme as the older couple left. Once the door was closed and their footsteps descended the staircase, Colt turned Esme in his arms. "Is there anything we need to do now?"

Esme looked up at him, a coy smile on her face. "That depends on your definition of 'need.'"

"Well, wife, I think there is something we need to do." His hands slid up her back under her shirt. "How about we try out that bed?"

"I think that's a pressing need. Don't you?"

Colt's kiss was his answer.

CHAPTER SIXTEEN

Aaron's smile welcomed Esme when she entered the emergency department her first shift back at work. She'd only been gone a week, four of those days being her regular days off. It seemed like much longer with everything that had happened during the week.

"Hey, girl. How are you doing?" Aaron gave her a hug.

Esme smiled. "I'm great. You?" She knew her face reflected her joy. It didn't take Aaron long to pick up on the fact that something had occurred.

"Okay, so tell me what's going on? You're way too happy for someone whose ex was here a few days ago."

"Well…" Esme held up her left hand, wiggling her fingers. "I'm now Mrs. Colt Sawyer."

A shriek came from the office behind them. "What? You got married?" Gretchen flew into the hall where Esme and Aaron stood.

"Uh huh." It was all she could say with her face pressed against Gretchen as she was hugged tightly.

When her co-worker released her and grabbed her hand to study the rings, Esme said, "Colt was so very sweet. He took such care with me when we left that day." She went on to explain how Colt proposed and how they decided to fly to Vegas and get married. "I wasn't sure about it until he listened to my concerns and said he didn't want to pressure me. If I wanted to wait, we would. That's when I knew. He's going to be there supporting and protecting me always."

"Hey, girl," Gretchen said. "After what you did to that attacker in the parking lot, I think you're pretty good at protecting yourself."

Esme grinned at her. "Yeah, maybe. Besides, I can swing a pretty good baseball bat."

"What?" Gretchen asked.

"Didn't I ever tell you how I met Colt?"

Aaron laughed. "It's a pretty good story."

The trio went into the office, and Esme explained as she stowed her purse. She smoothed her floral scrubs.

"My apartment has video monitors of all the cameras around the building," Esme explained. "I saw this strange man in the gym. I have this baseball bat I bought for protection. I snuck downstairs and into the gym. Colt turned just as I swung the bat. He caught it, which probably saved him from a concussion."

"You didn't." Gretchen's mouth was open in shock.

"I did."

"You're a force to be reckoned with. Does your ex know you're lethal? Have you registered with the FBI as a deadly weapon?" Gretchen lifted her hands in the classic karate pose.

Esme laughed. "No, and don't you tell him."

The radio beeped, signaling a report from an ambulance crew. Aaron went to answer it. "Time for work, ladies."

"I'm happy for you, Esme," Gretchen said.

"Thanks. I'm happy too."

"I MAY HAVE TO BREAK DOWN AND START WEARING THAT spring foot," Colt said. "It's just too hot to wear long pants to jog in. Between the sleeve for the prosthetic and the pant leg, I'm sweating. Shorts would be much more comfortable."

He and Rigs were jogging the River Walk. It was early in the morning since the summer weather was hot. Both men had left their wives sleeping to meet and get their ten miles in before they worked out. Once their exercise was complete, they'd go home for breakfast meeting again later to start their work-day.

They'd already completed one circuit of the walk and were getting ready to cross the bridge over the Arkansas River as it went through town. The old bridge didn't allow motorized vehicles and was a popular place with its park areas on either end.

Both men stopped when their phones sounded an alarm. A security system had been set off. Each man looked at their phone before looking at each other. The building indicating a break-in was Peris Security Systems.

They didn't jog. They ran. There was only one person they thought might try to get into the building. Hugo. And Esme was alone in the apartment.

ESME REACHED OUT. SHE OPENED HER EYES. COLT WASN'T in bed with her. Looking at the clock, she realized he was out jogging with Rigs. She stretched, reaching above her head with clasped hands.

"Coffee, brush teeth, shower, not necessarily in that order," she muttered. Esme crawled out of bed, made it, and headed into the bathroom. With two on the list completed, she dressed in her flamingo scrubs.

"Coffee. Please have made coffee, Colt." Esme left the bedroom sniffing. "I love you. You made coffee before you left."

As she was reaching for the coffee pot, a beeping came from the security monitors. Esme ran to the wall covered with the screens. Two had indicator lights flashing. One was an outside view of the back door to the building. The other was the inside view. Someone had triggered the alarm. Neither monitor showed anyone.

Esme flicked her gaze to the video of the hallway that bisected the building front to back. Her heart began pounding. Hugo was striding toward the stairs.

Esme froze. She was alone. He'd come for her. When he found out she was married, he'd kill her. She knew it.

Her chest tightened. Panic flooded in, stealing her breath. She watched as he turned into the stairwell. He disappeared from the monitor.

Suddenly, Esme could breathe again. Thoughts began flying through her mind. SING. No, there was no way she was going to let him get that close to her. Gretchen's comment that she was a lethal force. A deadly weapon. Her baseball bat!

Esme ran to the corner where the bat leaned against the wall. Grabbing it, she ran to stand just behind where the door would swing open. No way was she going to let him get into the apartment. No way was she going to let him get near her.

Straining to hear, Esme listened for his footsteps. The old building creaked. The fifth step from the top squeaked. Hugo was near the top.

Esme glanced at the door. Colt had locked it when he left, but the slide bolts couldn't be locked from the outside. She didn't have time to slide them. Esme could hear a pick working in the lock.

She lifted the bat, ready to swing.

The door opened slowly. Hugo stepped in, surveying the room. Just as he turned his head her direction, Esme swung.

COLT BURST THROUGH THE BACK DOOR AND RAN DOWN the hall. There was a crashing sound coming from the staircase. He heard Esme screaming. Turning into the stairwell, he stopped.

Hugo lay in a heap at the bottom, clutching his right arm. Esme stood at the top yelling.

"Take that. You come after me again, and I'll do worse to you. I've taken down another creep just like I did you. Show your face around me again and you'll hurt even more." She noticed Colt. "Look what I did. I got him. I got him. Call the cops. He's violated the Order of Protection. He broke into the building. I smacked him good with the bat when he tried to get into the apartment." She kept up a stream of words while he looked down at Hugo.

"You're just stupid aren't you?" Colt asked. "You break into the building with the most surveillance cameras. A state of the art security system. And my wife who has a baseball bat and knows how to use it."

Hugo just looked at him, clutching his arm that had an extra bend in it between the wrist and elbow. There was a lump forming near his eye, where the bat must have clipped him as he shielded his face by lifting his arm.

"The police are on their way. Is Esme okay?" Rigs came up behind Colt.

Colt looked up the stairs. Esme was cautiously descending, her bat ready to swing again. The enclosed stairway was narrow, but he figured, with her hyped on adrenalin, she'd figure a way.

"She's fine." Colt stepped as far to the side as he could in the small space to allow Rigs to stick his head in and look.

"Yeah, she's good," Rigs said. "Hey, Esme. Good job. You want to give me the bat now?"

"Nope, not until this SOB is locked up in a squad car." She wiggled the bat above her shoulder. She eyed Hugo. "They'll take you to the ER before they book you. Guess what. I'm on duty in an hour. You want me to treat you?" She waved the bat again. The look in her eyes said she relished the thought.

Hugo looked from Esme to the men. "You keep her away from me. She's crazy. She broke my arm and knocked me down the stairs."

Esme let out a slightly hysterical laugh. "I'll do worse than that. I can swing this bat and hit you in very vulnerable places. I know all of them on a body."

Hugo turned onto his knees, struggling to get up. Colt and Rigs grabbed his upper arms and hauled him into the hall.

Rigs twisted Hugo's left arm around to his back. "Come on. We'll just wait for the police over here." He pulled him toward the lobby as the sound of sirens could be heard approaching.

Colt stepped into the stairwell. "Esme, Sweets. You were wonderful. Give me the bat now, please."

"I got him. Did you see? I got him. Knocked him totally down the stairs. Now, he knows I'm not to be messed with. The police will take him away for good now, won't they?" The bat she was holding high over her shoulder lowered a bit.

"Yes, they'll take him away." Colt stepped on the first step. Esme moved down one.

"He knows he can't mess with me anymore, right?"

"He knows you're able to protect yourself."

She blinked, and the frenzied look left her eyes. Lowering the bat, Esme said, "I can, can't I?"

Colt closed the distance between them and took the bat. He set it on a step and wrapped his arms around her. She was trembling. "Yes, you can, and did."

Esme clung to him. He stroked her hair as she began shaking. Sobs broke through and soaked his shoulder.

CHAPTER SEVENTEEN

ESME HELD COLT'S HAND AS THEY LISTENED TO THE JUDGE pronounce the sentence. Hugo was going to prison for a long time. The judge wasn't being lenient. The vast amount of video evidence showing Hugo from the moment he stepped onto Rigs' property to Hugo being led out of the building and placed in a squad car simplified the case.

There hadn't even been a jury trial. Hugo's lawyer urged him not to waste the court's time and to plead guilty. Maybe the judge would appreciate not having to sit through all the steps involved with a jury trial for such an open and shut case. From the length of the sentence, she hadn't taken that into consideration when she'd given him the maximum time for his crimes.

"Mr. Braga, you'd do well to spend your time

reflecting on the proper way to treat a woman. Your actions toward Mrs. Sawyer demonstrate a selfishness and disregard for the rights and safety of another person that is totally unacceptable. Along with your prison time, the Order of Protection for Mrs. Sawyer will stand in effect once you are released. If you come within miles of her when you are released, you will be back in prison. Do I make myself clear?"

Hugo nodded. He never looked at Esme. His arm was in a cast. The break had required surgery, complete with pins and plates.

"Bailiff, take Mr. Braga out of my courtroom." The judge pounded her gavel and watched Hugo be hand-cuffed and led away.

Those in the courtroom were silent as the judge studied something on her bench. She looked up, straight at Esme. "Mrs. Sawyer. Please approach the bench."

Esme looked at Colt and rose. She slipped from behind the table and walked forward. What could the woman want to say to her? She stood a few feet from the tall platform the judge sat on and twisted her hands together.

A soft smile transformed the serious expression on the judge's face into a compassionate one. "Don't be nervous, Mrs. Sawyer. I just want to say I'm sorry you had to go through your experiences with Mr. Braga. The previous complaint you filed against him should have resulted in a stiffer penalty. Maybe if it had, he would have thought better of coming after you. Hopefully, he will take my words to heart and leave you in peace."

"I hope so, Your Honor."

"I have something here I'll return to you. Although I'm not a fan of violence, sometimes it's necessary. Your method of protecting yourself may be unusual, but it worked. Well done." The judge lifted Esme's baseball bat that had been submitted as evidence and handed to her.

"Thank you."

"One more thing," said the judge. "I hear a rumor that you received one of the messages on the Java Cupid cups. Is this true?"

Esme's eyes went wide. How had she found out? "Yes, ma'am. It said, *'My love will always protect you.'*"

The judge looked from Esme to Colt and back. "Seems to me you can protect yourself, but I'm glad you have someone who loves you and wants to do the same."

"I am too, Your Honor. Thank you."

As they left the courtroom, Colt drew her to the side of the hallway. He wrapped his arms around Esme and said, "The judge is right. You can protect yourself. And where you can't, I will."

Esme's smile was bright as she nodded.

A NOTE FROM SOPHIE

I hope you enjoyed **Java Protect**. Please take a moment to leave a review on Amazon. For independently publishing authors like myself, the reviews are extremely valuable in getting our work noticed. If you take just a few minutes you could help someone else find their next favorite book.

If you'd like to be notified of upcoming releases, please sign up for my newsletter. It only comes to you when there is actual real news about my books.

Thank you!
Sophie

ABOUT THE AUTHOR

Sophie Dawson is an award-winning author of fictional romance, both historical and contemporary. An eclectic conglomeration of interests and accomplishments, she has made up stories in her head all her life. Now she types them out. Her critically acclaimed series include Cottonwood, Stones Creek, and Love's Infestation. She's also been part of several multi-author projects, including Silverpines and Pinkerton Matchmaker.

BOOKS BY SOPHIE DAWSON

Cottonwood Series

Healing Love

Lord's Love

Giving Love

Redeeming Love (With George McVey)

Stones Creek Series

Leah's Peace

Chasing Norie

Chloe's Choice (Short Story)

Chloe's Sanctuary

Ladies of Sanctuary House

Laundry Lady's Love

Music of Her Heart

His Protective Wings

Silverpines (shared series)

Wanted: Shopkeeper (Silverpines Book 4)

Wanted: Bookkeeper (Silverpines Book 14)

Wanted: Developer (Silverpines Book 24)

Pinkerton Matchmaker (shared series)

An Agent for Wilhelmina (Pinkerton Matchmaker Book 4)

An Agent for Delaney (Pinkerton Matchmaker Book 16)

Lockets and Lace (shared series)

Pearl's Will (Lockets and Lace Book 9)

Driving Lillian (Lockets and Lace Book 17)

www.ingramcontent.com/pod-product-compliance
Lightning Source LLC
Chambersburg PA
CBHW070324130626
46556CB00007B/2721